# MURDER IN BOSTON'S NORTH END

A Plot Twist Cozy Mystery

Massachusetts Cozy Mystery

ANDREA KRESS

# Chapter 1

Amanda Burnside had not been looking forward to her dinner with Doctor Fred Browne because of the conversation that would invariably ensue. He had made attempts at proposing marriage to her before, and she had deflected the discussion, but lately he had become impatient with her reluctance to make a commitment.

From her perspective, marriage to a doctor from a good family was precisely what was expected of a single woman in her twenties in Boston. But it wasn't what Amanda wanted. She was hard put to articulate what she did want, except it ought to challenge her intelligence and skills and, frankly, she thought being a society wife was not that and boring to boot. She had spent the recent past volunteering at Mercy Hospital and then working on a part-time basis designing the reception area for the Indigent Children's Clinic. That task had morphed into another project with the Mayor's blessing: an auxiliary clinic in Boston's North End. She knew the motivation on his part had more to do with garnering votes with the mostly Italian population than pure altruism. But that didn't matter to her because the decision had served both their purposes. The Mayor would surely get goodwill from his gesture, and Amanda would have something to do every day besides having lunch with friends and shopping.

Fred was fiddling with his silverware and looking down at his empty plate, a sure sign that he was not only uncomfortable but reluctant to face the response to the question both knew was coming. In an attempt to relieve the tension, Amanda began to brightly tell him the progress of her new project.

"I have to say, the Sons of Italy group have been more than generous with their time and their contacts in getting the North End clinic off the ground. They've managed to raise funds to buy some of the equipment needed—such as the portable privacy screens—and one of the furniture store owners is donating chairs. Just think what I had to do to find chairs for the reception area back in the main clinic! All that bargaining with the owners and reducing the order to fit the budget. And here, the merchants come forward with donations without even being asked."

"That's political influence for you," Fred said.

"I hope you don't think that I somehow compromised the hospital or myself by accepting their generosity," she said.

"No, no. Not at all. It is for the greater good. And the notion that the medical residents will cycle through that clinic will give them needed experience."

"Have any of them objected to the proposal?"

"A few were hesitant about working so closely with the new immigrant population, but they must realize that we serve everyone. Our country is still so new that everyone is a few generations from being an immigrant."

"True enough," Amanda said, knowing her mother would be horrified at her admission. After all, her family saw themselves as the original population of New England since they didn't consider the Indians in that equation.

The waiter brought their plates of food, Fred forgoing the usual appetizers, salad or soup, which was a relief to Amanda. It meant the meal would be short and the difficult discussion brought to an end sooner.

Fred was halfway through his cutlet when he suddenly said, "Amanda, I can't keep this to myself any longer." He put down his fork and knife and looked directly into her eyes. "I would like you to be my wife and I would, with all due respect, like an answer this evening. Not tomorrow or next week or put off any longer."

Amanda set her cutlery down as well. "I feel it my responsibility to tell you that I admire you greatly and I appreciate your attention and patience. But even after all the while we have known each other, I am not ready to be married." As an afterthought, she said, "Although I do wish you well."

He picked up his utensils and resumed cutting a portion of meat from the bone. After slowly chewing and swallowing, he said, "I thought that might be your answer." He looked down at his plate and continued eating.

Was that it, Amanda wondered? Shouldn't he have wiped a tear from his eye or got down on his knees and begged her to reconsider? No, that was not Fred—and that was part of the problem. Sometimes she felt as if he considered the act of choosing a wife some kind of transaction based on careful evaluation of the facts. She was young, educated, attractive, lively, and of a good family. That ticked off many of his requirements. But there was no passion on his part and therefore no reciprocal emotion on hers. That was a necessary condition for her to even consider marrying someone. What about love?

She didn't say anything and resumed eating, hoping that the silence would not last too much longer. However, it did, so she brought out her cheerful voice to tell him more of the latest work developments.

"The women in the neighborhood have been so welcoming, too. Several have decided that I am too thin and need to eat more pasta and bread. And have even volunteered to teach me how to cook their food."

"They're just trying to fix you up with one of their handsome sons, full of fire and emotion," Fred said. He looked up at her. "Sorry, I shouldn't have said that."

She paused and thought it was a strange thing to say in response to her comment, but he wasn't far off the mark. It seemed to be the general frame of mind of those women that their husbands might be a handful but better than a cold fish, as one of them had characterized American men.

"Were you planning on going skiing this winter?" she asked in an obvious change of direction.

"I don't know if I can get away anytime soon. This idea of the additional clinic will likely blossom into a host of others, and I'll be hard pressed to juggle the staff around to accommodate the load."

"I'm sorry if I seemed to have spoiled things for you," she said.

He put down his utensils again and, with elbows on the table, steepled his hands in front of his face. "I really do apologize, Amanda. I have been behaving very badly. I'm acting like a selfish, jilted boyfriend." He smiled a bit crookedly. "Well, I am a selfish, jilted boyfriend."

He reached across the table and grasped one of her hands. "It was wonderful while it lasted."

She sighed. She would never say it aloud, but it hadn't been all that wonderful. Peaceful, predictable and safe were better descriptions of their relationship. She was still looking for something more exciting in her life and a partner who could rouse her emotions.

Amanda couldn't know that she was about to encounter both.

## Chapter 2

With Amanda and her father busy with work, her mother occupied with charity work and running the household and Louisa allegedly attending classes, it was seldom that the entire family had breakfast together. But this day was a rare occasion that led to many questions directed at Amanda about Fred.

"Well, dear, where did you go for dinner last night?" her mother asked.

"One of his favorite old-fashioned chop places with excellent food and grumpy, old waiters."

"Ah, that's often where you find the best food in Boston," her father said. "I'm guessing the one in the financial district."

"Exactly."

There was a brief silence before her mother inquired, "Well?"

"Well, what?" Amanda asked as innocently as she could manage.

Her mother exhaled in frustration that her daughters never seemed to want to share information about their beaux. She rather hoped that Louisa wouldn't share about hers, a man who was several years older than her daughter and who owned a nightclub, of all things. She had met him before at the beach house in Maine and he appeared intelligent and gallant, but still....

"No, Mother, we are not engaged. And in fact, we have sort of broken things off."

"Sort of!" her mother said a bit loudly.

"He's a nice fellow, sincere, hard-working, but...."

"No SA," said Louisa with a smirk.

"What does that mean?" her mother asked.

Louisa didn't dare tell her it stood for sex appeal, so she made something up. "Sense awareness," she added.

Her mother looked puzzled and her father askance at what he suspected was not the actual meaning. "One of the terms you have learned in your social work classes?" he asked.

"Why, yes. Every state of mind and emotion gets classified. It's very interesting." She tried to stifle a smile.

"That sounds very tiresome," Mrs. Burnside said. "Putting people's feeling in a box with a label on it."

The doorbell rang and Nora could be seen traversing the sitting room beyond to answer it.

"It's awfully early. I hope it's not a telegram about some bad news," said Mrs. Burnside, an inveterate worrier.

Louisa stretched her neck to see around the door from the breakfast room but gave up. A moment later, Nora stepped in to say, "Miss Louisa, there has been a delivery for you."

She jumped up from the table and Mrs. Burnside followed.

"Good Heavens!" she was heard to exclaim from the sitting room. There was nothing else to do but see what the commotion was about, and Amanda and her father dutifully followed. On the table in the center of the sitting room was an enormous bouquet of flowers, most of them out of season, in a large vase. Louisa was reading the note that had been attached, her cheeks growing pinker and her mother more curious by the moment. She held her hand out to her daughter, demanding to see the contents of the missive.

"Well, I never!" she said, handing it to her husband.

"Is this the Rob person who came up to the Beach House last summer?" he asked.

"Yes," Louisa answered calmly although her sister could tell she was nervous.

"What does this mean? Why has he sent you flowers?"

"He admires me," she said, trying to look nonchalant.

Amada stifled a scoffing noise and her sister glared at her.

"'*All my love?*' I would say that sounds more than admiration. And suspiciously as if has already been reciprocated to some degree."

"Oh, Daddy. It's just a turn of phrase."

The Burnsides senior looked at one another and nodded. "Back to the breakfast room," her father commanded. They followed and resumed their seats, but nobody took up a fork or knife.

"Your mother and I have been very concerned about you, Louisa. I blame myself for not having put my foot down earlier. And I am under the impression that you have continued to be in contact with this man despite our recommendations to the contrary." He looked at her, but her eyes were on her plate. He then looked at Amanda, the older of the two girls, who shrugged her shoulders in a plausible imitation of ignorance, although she knew that her sister had been sneaking out nearly every night to go to his club, the Oasis, to keep him company, as she said. Whatever else transpired, she didn't dare ask.

Mrs. Burnside spoke up. "I have to say that Mary asked me a question yesterday that quite surprised me. She asked how to clean a silk garment with sequins. Naturally, I couldn't imagine what she was talking about, and she mentioned it was one of your gowns, Louisa. Now, I certainly don't remember ever having ordered such a dress for you and I asked her to show me which one. Imagine my surprise when she led me to your closet to see this shocking array of evening gowns. Many of which were of very skimpy design," she added, looking at her husband.

"And where do you wear such garments?" her father demanded. "Surely not to class."

Louisa took a deep breath and finally said, "I go to the Oasis from time to time. I can hardly go in a tweed skirt and a twin set."

"You go to a nightclub?" her father practically shouted.

"Amanda has been there, too," she said in her defense.

All eyes swiveled toward Amanda, who glared at her sister.

"I was there once," she protested. "I went to make sure that it wasn't a den of iniquity, as you might have imagined. It's a high-class establishment, by the looks of it, no gangsters or crude people. The entertainment is quite good, and it doesn't serve alcohol." That last bit was a total fabrication, but she thought it was best not to mention it at the moment.

"That's it," her father said, slamming his hand down on the table. The family stared at the gesture that they had rarely witnessed.

"You have been pestering us about going to see your friends in Georgia or Florida or wherever for weeks. 'Can't stand the endless winter. All my friends are going. It won't cost you a thing.'"

"My friend Eunice is actually in Charleston, South Carolina," Louisa said.

"Well, you'll get your wish. You're going south for at least three weeks and you're not going to have any further contact with that nightclub fellow."

Louisa was suddenly conflicted. The prospect of having a vacation and being away from the scrutiny of her parents was tempting, but then she wouldn't be able to see Rob. And now that her mother was onto her escapades, when she did return, they would likely have her under total lockdown. She burst into tears.

"She has been nagging me since New Year's to get out of town and now that I've agreed, she's unhappy. What do you make of that, Margaret?" he said to his wife.

Louisa got up abruptly from the table and dashed out of the room.

"It's too bad I've got a job, or I would have been glad to act as chaperone for her trip," Amanda said. Her parents did not take her comment seriously. "Really," she added, hoping for their agreement.

"The both of you!" her father said, thrusting his napkin onto the table next to his half-eaten breakfast. He, too, left the room.

"Excuse me," Amanda said to her mother and went upstairs to see if Louisa's reaction was genuine or crocodile tears. She knocked softly on her sister's door but heard no answer.

She entered and found Louisa seated on her bed, sniffling.

"At least you got one thing you wanted," Amanda said.

"How could Mother go sneaking around into my closet!"

"It's probably not a good idea to accuse others of sneaking around."

Louisa turned her head away.

"Come on, you'll have fun, develop a delicious tan and everything will be the same when you come back."

Her sister refused to respond.

"You'll write letters—although I've never received one from you—and he'll send telegrams and flowers. Your friends will be jealous."

"What kind of fool is he to have sent a gigantic bouquet of flowers to my home?"

"A romantic one, I suppose. Let's get you packing. The sooner you're gone, the sooner you'll be back." Amanda went to the closet and hauled out a sizable suitcase from an upper shelf.

"You'll need a bathing suit, I suppose," she began.

Louisa started to perk up at the thought of going to a beach in late January rather than flitting about Boston at night in an evening gown and coat trying to stay warm and not ruin her shoes in the slush.

"I just have to make a short phone call," she said and left Amanda to open the blanket chest where Louisa stored her off-season clothes. There was a cute, two-piece outfit with a red and white striped top and loose white pants. That would look good sauntering across the veranda of wher-ever she was going and a jaunty beret in a matching red that would show off her blond hair to advantage. She pawed through the pile of clothes and heard Louisa's return.

"Very clever," she said. "Rob did *not* send those flowers."

Amanda stared at her sister.

"But I think I know who did."

# Chapter 3

Mr. Burnside had acted quickly that morning, calling the father of the girl who had issued the invitation to Louisa, the mother and aunt having accompanied her daughter and another girl as chaperones. His secretary was charged with going to the Central Station to buy a ticket to New York City where Louisa could spend the night at his brother's home north of the city. Said brother would then accompany her back to Manhattan early the next morning with a ticket to Charleston, a long day's journey, where she'd be retrieved by her friend's family.

It took him most of the morning to get things ready, including a stack of cash for the trip, and yet he still worried that he had overlooked something. He told his secretary to hold his personal calls for the remainder of the day; he had a nagging feeling that his wife would call to persuade him to change his mind and keep Louisa at home. But he knew that trying to corral the girl would be nearly impossible and just lead to more arguments. Best that she get over her romance far from home and perhaps meet someone more socially acceptable while she was away.

Amanda had agreed to set up a meeting with the Mayor's aide, Henry Rogers, at the hospital so he could see how the original clinic, still in renovation mode, had been set up and look at the drawings for the proposed reception area. She also wanted him to observe how the interim clinic had been put together in a smaller space for comparison, so that he could remain open-minded about layouts for additional sites in the future.

"Let's go up to the North End and see how Hizzoner's project is coming along."

Amanda was puzzled for a moment. "Is that what you call him?" she asked.

He was a short fellow with light brown hair that was combed to enhance a deep wave on one side, and he carefully placed his hat on so as not to disturb it as they walked toward the parking lot.

"No, not to his face. It's a term they use in Chicago and New York, and I thought it would be swell if we started using it for our Mayor. Elevates the office, don't you think?"

She thought it sounded as if somebody was giving him the raspberries. "Aren't we better than those two cities? More refined?"

"Like the 'City on the Hill?'" he teased. "Say, how long have you been doing this job?" he asked as he let her open her own door to the car.

"I've been volunteering in a different capacity for about two years and just started doing this recently. The new hospital director, Mr. Barlow, was glad of the help."

"Yeah, I've heard about him." He put the car in gear and spun out of the lot quickly. "How do you think this new project is going?"

"I was surprised that the Sons of Italy acted so quickly to make it happen. Mr. De Luca was very helpful."

He chuckled. "No doubt. He wants to stay in the Mayor's good graces. And put a feather in his cap to boot."

"What do you mean?" she asked.

"He wants to deliver votes for the party and make sure that everybody knows who did it. He's very ambitious."

Amanda wondered what kind of reward he expected from smoothing the way for this but thought she would seem naïve if she asked.

"I've already suggested to the hospital Board that the original site be renamed 'Mercy Clinic' and not 'Indigent Children's Clinic.' They could follow suit with the new location, too.

After all, people don't have to prove they are poor to use the facilities, and some might not even show up if they feel they are branded in that way."

"Good thinking," he said.

"From a public health standpoint, the hospital should offer as many services as it can rather than restrict them."

Henry looked over at her with admiration. "And you could hardly ask people to prove their financial status before helping them. They'd either lie or take it the wrong way."

As they approached Hanover Street in the North End, Henry slowed down since there were more pedestrians, some of whom stepped off the curb into the street because the sidewalks were blocked by shop displays. One storekeeper stood in the doorway with an apron over his thick sweater and a snap-brimmed cap on his head, surveying the women who were looking over his vegetables. Henry waved at him, and he put his chin up in recognition.

"Do you come here a lot?" Amanda asked.

"Part of the job. Mingling with the constituents. Seeing what they need even if Sal De Luca thinks that is his job. It very well might be, but someone has to make sure that the favors folks are asking for are legit."

"How did you come to work for the Mayor?" she asked. His streetwise use of slang made him seem one step away from a hoodlum, but, of course, he could not be that. Perhaps the Mayor pulled him out of some reform school in an attempt at redemption.

"I majored in poli sci at Boston College and my project was on the organization of Boston's government. And I use the term loosely. When the Mayor ran for office, I asked if I could help, and the rest is history. All the big shots need folks like me as an intermediary. I'm a civil servant. And some days it feels like I'm just a plain old servant. Say, have you been to the North End before?"

"Certainly," she said. She didn't admit that it had only been to have dinner a few times with Fred. Why else would she venture into a neighborhood where she didn't know anyone?

"You'll get used to it. Pretty crowded nowadays. Mostly Italian, as if you didn't guess. Used to be Irish and before that probably German. The immigration really jumped up in the last few years with all the tumult in Europe."

She knew about the Great War having a major effect on peoples' lives, but she didn't know what else had happened since then and was too embarrassed to ask. She didn't need to, as he felt a compulsion to talk most of the time.

"We got the Depression, but those folks were already having a terrible time with their economies. What with the Russian revolution and those anarchists. You know what's funny? When you go through immigration coming into this country, they ask all kinds of questions, including are you an anarchist. As if you would admit it." He laughed. "But it does serve a purpose. Because if it turns out you are and you lied on your entry papers, poof," and here he stuck his thumb in the air and gestured while making a clicking noise. "You're out of here."

"How do you know these things?" she asked. She wondered if they taught this in college.

"People tell me stuff. Not in my poli sci classes, I can assure you. Folks on the street. Say, don't you watch the newsreels?"

Of course, she did. They preceded every movie that was shown. But she certainly didn't glean that kind of information from them.

"Here we are. Hey!" he shouted to another man on the sidewalk as he got out of the car, and they shook hands and threw their arms around each other with some banter she could not hear from inside the car. Since he wasn't polite enough to open the door for her, she did it herself.

"This your girlfriend?" the other man asked.

"Nah, she works at the hospital."

The other man, only slightly taller than Henry with a dark walrus moustache and heavy brows, looked at her with puzzlement. "You a nurse?" he asked.

"No, she works *for* the hospital," Henry explained.

His companion understood the words but had no idea what difference it made. Here was a tall woman, expensively dressed and not in a uniform. He might ask for an explanation later.

Henry walked quickly down the sidewalk but she was slower, fascinated by the stores they passed. A man's elegant three-piece suit hung on a mannequin in a haberdasher's shop next to a dressmaker's, similarly advertising her wares including a hat and gloves on a table at eye level. An open door to a stairway advertised that attorneys had their offices upstairs. In the window of a religious shop were statues, rosaries and small mannequins displaying a boy's white suit with short pants and a girl's dress with a white veil. Henry stopped and waited for her to catch up then gestured at the door of a bakery.

"That's First Communion stuff," he said. "Coming up in the spring. The first significant thing for the kids. And a big deal for the families, with parties thrown by the godparents."

Once the door to the bakery was opened, Amanda was enveloped in the sweet smell of cookies and pastries behind the glass counters.

"Let's have a coffee," he said, approaching the stout woman behind the counter.

"Two," he said, holding up two fingers unnecessarily. She went to the other end of the counter to a machine and clanked metal against metal before there were hissing sounds. Amanda was curious as to what she was doing, but Henry was urging her to select some cookies from the enormous selection before them.

"A lot of them are made from the same dough, just different shapes and colors."

She pointed at an S-shaped one and another tinted pink with sprinkles on top and waited for the woman to return with tiny cups of dark coffee. Armed with the cookies and the coffee, they sat at a round, marble-topped table. The woman came around and placed two short glasses of water alongside them and smiled.

Amanda took a sip and widened her eyes. She put the cup down. "Would it be impolite to ask for milk and sugar?"

Henry laughed. "I bet you're used to the bland American stuff."

"I think you must be right. One cup of this could probably keep me going all day."

He got up and made a request to the woman, who returned to their table with a tolerant smile and nod of the head.

"So let me tell you about what's going on here. As if you hadn't noticed, the Irish have come into positions of power in the city. Not just political power, but also financial and illegal activity."

Amanda looked surprised.

"Hey, I'm just telling it like it is. The Italians have come to dominate the North End and, as you might imagine, the political machine here. That's were Sal comes in. He gives favors to people and in return he suggests that they vote for certain candidates. He arranges small meetings with various people who are flattered that they are the select group to be seeing him and the Mayor one on one, except that they don't know that he does these over and over with many more people. That's how he builds what he calls his base. Those folks think they are special to have been singled out for their opinions and to be asked to donate money to the campaign."

"The money?" Amanda asked, never having thought about it before.

"Sure, how do you think it works?"

She didn't respond not wanting him to think she was naïve.

"Naturally it is all accounted for—pristine records. Campaign contributions are necessary in a democracy, but nobody is buying votes."

This was said so forcefully that Amanda decided not to ask any more questions but paid attention to the buttery cookie. She could see that Henry was studying her.

"What's your angle?"

"Pardon me?"

"What's your interest in the North End?"

"To put in a clinic as we have at Mercy Hospital. That's all."

He narrowed his eyes and then smiled. "Sure." He finished his espresso and looked at his watch. "You almost ready?"

She gulped down the coffee and wiped her mouth on one of the paper napkins provided while he paid the woman behind the counter.

"Where are we going?"

"To the Sons of Italy, of course!" He raised his fist in the air and the woman clapped in appreciation.

"Can you walk more slowly, please?" Amanda asked as they exited into the cold mid-morning. "I want to see everything." He looked a bit puzzled but soon saw that she wanted to take it all in, and he began to saunter beside her as she looked into each shop window they passed. It seemed every type of service or consumable was available without having to leave Hanover Street although she thought there must have been dozens of other streets in the neighborhood. Laundries, a funeral home, a fabric store, accountants, a butcher, until at last, they came to a larger building that stood apart from the others with a columned façade and two flags flying outside, one American and the other Italian.

Amanda held her hat onto her head in the wind as she looked up at the building, which could have passed for a bank or a post office.

"Impressive, no?"

"I'll say," Amanda said.

They climbed the stairs and Henry opened one of a pair of doors to enter a foyer then through another set of doors to an expansive room, elegantly decorated with a stage at one end.

"Welcome, welcome," came a voice out of the darkened room.

"Hey, Sal," Henry said, shaking his hand and clapping him on the back. "This is Amanda Burnside from the hospital."

"Mr. De Luca at your service," the tall man said, taking her hand and bowing slightly. "Please, come to my office." He ushered them toward the stage and then off to the left through a door and a hallway to a large office with big windows overlooking the street. He gestured for them to sit down.

"I wanted to meet you in person and thank you for all the work you have done so far to set up the clinic," Amanda said.

De Luca closed his eyes and shook his head. "Anything for my people. And for the Mayor, of course," he added.

"I think we might be ready to begin next week," she said.

"Well, then we must have the ribbon cutting very soon! Leave it up to me. Speeches, entertainment—."

"And, of course, the Mayor should be there. I'll have to check his calendar when I get back to the office," Henry said.

"Naturally. The Mayor and I are the best of friends. And I know he loves the people of this neighborhood as much as I do."

There was a knock on the open door of the office and a young man in a smart suit excused himself and whispered something in De Luca's ear that made the smile freeze on his face.

"Please excuse me, but something urgent has come up that I must deal with." He stood and extended his hand graciously, indicating the audience was over. Henry and Amanda thanked him.

"We'll be in touch," Henry said.

As they walked down the steps outside, Amanda said, "He seems like a very helpful ally."

"Don't be fooled. The guy is a snake. The Mayor can't stand him and the feeling is mutual. But politically, they need each other."

# Chapter 4

Amanda and Henry walked slowly back down Hanover Street to where he had parked his car, crossing small side streets as they went while she tried to take in everything on the opposite side. Over the street noise, the clopping of the hooves of the ragman's horse and the loud voices of people talking, she heard a scream. Startled, she turned to see where it had come from, but Henry didn't react.

"Just someone in an argument. You may have noticed that Italians are very vocal and expressive people."

The screaming continued and then even Henry looked concerned as several people peered down a narrow side street. They stood still and a policeman on foot came barreling past them and through the throng that was gathering to where it ran perpendicular to the wide alley. He looked both ways and dashed off to the right, with half the swarm of people following in his wake and the other half propelling Henry and Amanda through the dark street along with them. People were shouting, stumbling and shoving until they came to the back of a shop with broken windows and a man lying on the ground halfway out of the doorway. The woman by his side had stopped screaming and was overcome with sobbing as she clutched his lifeless head to her breast.

"Make way! Make way!" the policeman shouted although he could barely get through the mass of men and women who surrounded what looked like mother and son. It seemed everyone in the crowd had something to say or yell to their neighbors or to the woman on her knees.

The policeman blew his whistle, and the crowd was quiet. "Move away! Let's see if anything can be done."

Amanda had been pushed closer to the side of the alley and her feet crunched on the broken glass. She turned to look into the back of the shop and saw broken saints' statues and Madonnas with chunks of plaster strewn across the floor inside.

People began to move back, and it was then that Amanda could see the man's white shirt, sleeves rolled up and the blood that soaked the left part of his chest. Henry appeared out of the crowd and grabbed her arm to pull her away, but she was mesmerized by the scene in front of her and couldn't move.

More police whistles were heard, and the crowd parted to let through two men in plainclothes who dashed to the side of the young man. Amanda stood on tiptoes to see what was going on and was surprised to see that one of the newcomers was Detective Halloran. She didn't think he worked in this part of the city since she had last encountered him in connection with the events on Boston Common. He was accompanied by a shorter fellow with dark hair and the two of them looked around, shouting, asking if anyone had witnessed the deed.

No one spoke. The people at the perimeter of the crowd melted away, leaving only a handful of people, near neighbors or friends by the degree of familiarity they showed to the woman keening on the ground.

"I'm sorry, he's dead," Halloran said.

The other detective repeated the phrase in Italian for the woman, who by that time had fully realized it.

"Did anyone see anything?" Halloran asked and each person in the small group shook their head. "And what are you doing here?" he asked, looking in Amanda's direction.

She stammered and Henry came to the rescue. "We just left a meeting at the Sons of Italy and heard the screaming. We came to see what the matter was."

Halloran glared at both of them. "Don't leave," he commanded, holding up his index finger, his blue eyes blazing.

Next, he addressed the man who had come with him. "Find someone to take her home while we wait for the ambulance."

A woman stepped forward and volunteered but was swatted away by the mourning mother.

"Her grief must be intolerable," Amanda muttered.

"Yes, but she and that neighbor have been feuding for years. Can't let go of a good feud," Dominic, the other detective said.

Halloran asked, "Who is he?" and when no one responded, his colleague offered an opinion.

"I think he and his father own the Saint Lorenzo Gift Shop that fronts onto Hanover. This is their workshop."

Halloran stepped around to look inside the back of the shop without touching the doorway and said, "It looks like a robbery. Where's the father?"

A yell was heard from the far end of the alley and an older man came running, his shirt not fully stuffed into his pants as he pulled his suspenders over his shoulders. He was shouting and crying and fell to his knees next to the woman and they both sobbed.

"I guess that's him. If the kid was left alone in the shop, he must have been taken by surprise."

It was some time before an ambulance arrived and had to park on Hanover with two attendants bringing a stretcher into the alley. By that time, most of the crowd had dispersed and the mother had put her apron over her son's face.

"You take him to the funeral home, no?" the father asked.

"I'm sorry we can't," Dominic replied. "If this is a murder, we must take him to the morgue and do an autopsy."

The mother and father stood up and let out a stream of Italian, shaking their fists at Dominic, gesturing and crying all at once. He took it quietly and it wasn't until Halloran intervened that they stopped. Dominic apologized in English and Italian to the couple, who watched their son's body taken up by the attendants and then out of sight down the side street. Then they slowly walked back down the alley to an apartment building toward the end and disappeared. Halloran's colleague began to follow them but was shooed off by the father.

"Shouldn't we do something for them?" Amanda asked. "Where are the rest of their family and friends?"

"It's a complicated situation," Dominic responded. "They're from a different region from many of the folks here, and people think they are stuck up."

"But they're all Italians," Amanda pursued.

"The old country allegiances and stereotypes endure," Halloran said. "Like Northern Ireland and the Republic. Protestant and Catholic."

She shook her head that such things still mattered.

"We need to talk to the parents," Halloran said, "But first, let's check out the store."

"I'd better take you back to your office," Henry said.

They walked slowly back to Hanover Street to see the ambulance attendants just shutting the back doors of the vehicle and the small crowd still watching intently.

"I'd appreciate it if you wouldn't mention this to Mr. Barlow or the hospital Board members," Henry said.

"No, I hadn't thought of doing that. But they will read it in the newspapers anyway."

He stopped and looked at her. "This won't get in the newspapers."

"Because the Mayor will intervene and make sure it doesn't?"

"No, because no newspaper is interested in what goes on in the back alleys of the North End. There's plenty of crime to cover in the rest of the city."

Amanda was stunned by his candor and didn't want to believe him. Tomorrow, she was going to buy several newspapers that her family did not subscribe to and check to make sure that Henry was wrong. She simply couldn't believe that a young man's life didn't mean anything.

"Listen, there's more going on here than you can imagine. There are people here in this country who support the new regime in Italy and others who are dead set against it. It's not that they are all royalists—no, there are socialists, communists, unionists and anarchists who are not in favor of it. Who knows what political bent that young man had? Or if that had anything to do with it. Maybe it was just a robbery gone wrong, but your policemen friends will find out soon enough. It's best if you don't ask too many questions."

Halloran and Dominic were at that very moment searching the store. The back workshop was in disarray, with broken statues and plaster on the floor along with a blood stain.

"Looks like he got stabbed back here."

They moved to the front of the store and found that door unlocked, usual for most of the shops, and opening it struck the small bell above the head jamb.

"If the assailant had come in the front way and the young man was in the back, he would have been made aware of it. No blood on the floor here, however. The assailant could have come in the rear and may or may not have been seen by the victim."

"What do you think about the broken window?" Dominic asked.

They went out the back door and saw the shards on the ground.

"Maybe the back door was locked, and someone broke the window to get in. Or maybe the door was unlocked, and someone smashed into the window during their fight since most of the glass is in the alley," Halloran said.

Dominic walked outside and his shoes crunched on the glass. "Interesting." He looked at the buildings across the street but the shades or curtains on the windows were closed. "Doesn't mean someone didn't see something," he muttered. "Must have been some fight. Look at that mess back there," Dominic said as he straddled the back and front rooms. He looked around at the crowded shop with its missals, statues, rosaries, holy water fonts, calendars, scapulae, saints' pictures, crucifixes, medallions and every possible thing a good Catholic would want to purchase.

"Possible. We should go to the morgue and see if there are any wounds or bruises on his hands."

The little bell above the door tinkled and they stared at the tall, barrel-chested man who entered.

"Sorry, the shop is closed." Halloran said.

"Of course. I just wanted to see if I could help. I'm Salvatore De Luca," he said to Halloran. "I heard about the sad event. Is Giovanni dead?"

"Yes. How do you know what happened?"

"I have an interest in keeping the neighborhood safe. Johnny was a good boy. A little hotheaded, but nobody should have killed him. Plenty of young men have tempers around here. Old men, too," he added. He looked at Dominic then looked away.

"What do you know of the family? Did they have any trouble here?"

"Not that I know of. They have a good business. Look at the place!" De Luca said, venturing to the back of the shop. Halloran held out his arm to stop him.

"It's still a crime scene. We've just begun to look around and wouldn't like people trampling around what might be evidence."

The man held up both hands in a sign of surrender and gave a small smile. "Let me know if you need anything. If there's something I can do." He nodded and left.

Halloran looked at Dom. "How did he get here so quickly?"

"Bad news travels fast," he responded. "And that guy hears everything."

They heard the back door open and rushed to stop anyone else from entering. But it was the father who had come back, probably to survey the damage and make sure nothing was stolen. He shook his head at the loss of inventory before he saw the blood on the floor and stepped away toward the wall.

"Mister, er,"

"Rinaldi. I own the store."

"Yes, we figured that. Could you check the cash register and see if any money was taken."

He moved around them to the counter, which afforded a broad view of the street and anyone approaching, lifted the hatch that formed a boundary between the store and whatever was behind the counter and rang open the register. He flipped through the bills and the coins and shut the drawer.

"There's still money in there but some may have been taken. I won't know until I do the accounts."

"Did your son have any enemies?" Halloran asked.

"No! He was a good boy, worked in the store every day. He did some of the plaster casts for the saints and did a good job painting them. See?" He had moved out from behind the counter and picked up a Saint Anthony. "Look at that workmanship."

"Do you make all these yourself?" Halloran asked.

"All except the Madonnas. Those we import from Italy. There's a special workshop outside of Palermo—not that I'm Sicilian—but they have a good product at a good price. Every home must have a Madonna."

"Naturally," Halloran agreed. "Someone named De Luca was just in here asking if we needed any help."

"Pah!" the owner responded. "He's always sticking his nose in where it's not wanted. Thinks he is the big shot around here."

"Isn't he?" Halloran asks.

"No. No. The gangs, those are the real big shots. Everybody has to do what they say or else. It was bad enough when the Irish gang controlled everything, but you'd think a countryman would give you a break." He stopped suddenly, realizing that Halloran was Irish and that he was talking too much.

"Protection?"

"It's just something I heard. I'm upset. I don't know what I'm saying."

"So, the Italian gang wants protection money, too? Probably at a higher rate than the old gang that got driven out of here."

"I don't know anything about that. Nothing about nothing. I just want you to find out who killed my Giovanni. I won't rest until you find out." He locked the front door, put a CLOSED sign up and pulled a shade down.

"Where were you this morning?" Halloran asked.

"I didn't feel well and stayed home. If only I had gone to the store with him. He turned to go, then faced them again. "His mother…." He waved his hand in frustration at not being able to express his anger and grief.

"We'll need to talk to you both."

"Tomorrow. Please." The tears were streaming down the man's face, and he could barely get the words out.

# Chapter 5

The two detectives found their car and drove to the morgue to view the body in more detail. The Medical Examiner probably wouldn't get to their victim until the next day, depending on the workload, but they wanted to make sure to look at the body before the clothes were removed or anything else was touched. They stood in the empty waiting room for a few minutes before the skinny guy who logged in the incoming bodies came down the hall, his white lab coat open and flapping around his legs.

"We're here to see Giovanni Rinaldi."

"Geez, you guys are like ambulance chasers," he said. "They just brought him in a little while ago."

"We know, we were at the scene just after it happened."

"Doc is back there already giving him the once over." He stepped behind the counter and, still standing, shuffled papers around. "Go on back if you want," he said, not looking up.

They went through the double doors and peered through the windows of two rooms before locating Doctor Lindforth leaning over the body of a young man. He raised his head and looked over the rim of his glasses as the two men entered.

"This your man?" he asked.

They nodded.

"Pretty young." He shook his head. "What these people do to each other. I can't get to him until later today." He scratched the balding part of his head.

"We were at the scene after it happened. We just wanted to see if he was in a fight or was surprised by his assailant. He was alone in his family's shop and there was either a scuffle or fight but the place was wrecked."

"All right." He looked at Dominic and said, "Don't touch anything."

He didn't catch the glare that Dominic gave him in return as he bent over the body and, using the eraser end of a pencil, pushed the rolled-up sleeves farther up the young man's arms. He then bent over to look at the hands and the two detectives drew closer to observe.

"No bruises on the hands, no defensive wounds, either. He's a strong young man, yet he didn't fight back. Must have been surprised by the attacker."

"What's that red mark on his neck?" Halloran asked.

Using a probe, the M.E. pushed the collar to the side. "Looks like someone yanked on the chain." Pulling the shirt open, he revealed the gold chain with a crucifix and a horn-shaped pendant hanging from it. "Hmm," he said.

"Hmm, what?" Halloran asked.

"I don't know what to make of the chain being pulled. Maybe it was hanging out of his shirt and the assailant pulled him closer by pulling on it. Then knifed him."

"Or tried to pull it loose after he was knifed? As a thief might?"

"Both good explanations. If you two were at the scene, you might be able to make sense of all this. Whoever did it knew exactly where to put the blade."

AMANDA SAT in her small office on the hospital's tenth floor, tidying the papers in front of her but replaying the discovery of the body of the young man and the anguished parents who had raced to his side. She had a desperate need to tell someone about it but knew there was no one in whom to confide. Mr. Barlow would be horrified at what had taken place and probably wouldn't think it was some one-off event. If Henry was correct, although it was hard to separate his bluster from the facts, this violence was a commonplace thing that didn't even attract the attention of the newspapers. She couldn't imagine a shopkeeper in Beacon Hill suffering such an end and its going without notice. That's why she knew she couldn't tell her family. Certainly not Louisa, who would manage to manipulate it to her advantage. Nor her parents who would rein in any further activities she had there. Nor the X-D's, her fellow ex-debutantes who maintained their relationships with a monthly luncheon where the conversation was about what each one was doing, whom they were seeing, who was engaged, who was traveling and other such nonsense. She could just imagine their reaction if, after the first course at Valerie's club, she piped up with, "Oh, by the way. I've just encountered another murder. And you'll never guess where."

No. She was going to clam up, as the movie gangsters put it. No one was going to know about her presence at the scene or the terribly white face of what must have once been a robust and handsome young man.

Halloran knew, of course, and she meant to ask him what he was doing cruising around the North End with a sidekick in tow. She had been just as surprised to see him as he was to see her. Amanda hoped he didn't count her as some kind of witness, even if she arrived after the fact, along with a number of neighbors and passersby.

"Amanda?"

Lost in thought, she nearly jumped out of her chair. Then, putting her hand to her throat, she said, "Sorry, Mr. Barlow, you startled me."

He chuckled. "I apologize. I wanted to get a report from you about your trip this morning and how things are going with the new location."

"Certainly," she said. "I think your office would be more comfortable. Let me just get my things together."

He retreated and she felt she had to reach far back in her memory before the murder, all of which seemed so long ago. She picked up the papers in front of her to have something to hold onto and a notebook to record his reactions and walked down the hall, past Miss Bailey's clattering typewriter.

"It must have been a full morning for you, what with listening to the endless chatter of Henry Rogers," he said as she sat down.

She managed a smile. "He's very entertaining and knowledgeable, if one is to believe much of what he says."

"He's one of those young politicos who likes to show off how worldly he is, although contrary to the image he projects, I suspect he goes home to his mother in some leafy suburb each night rather than hanging out in a smoke-filled room with former operatives listening to their war stories."

"He did introduce me to espresso, and I think it has given me enough energy to last the entire day. We went to meet with Salvatore De Luca, who assured us that he was instrumental in making the new location possible. He didn't come out and say it, but he implied it was he, not the Mayor, who made it happen."

Mr. Barlow closed his eyes and shook his head. "It doesn't matter to me who made it happen. Let them fight over that bone between them. We'll stay out of it and get the work done."

"This is what he, or the Mayor's staff, managed to get done so far. The facility is enormous, and the first floor is used for meetings and social events. Very glamorous. I didn't get to see the upper floors, however. The clinic will be in the basement, where I was told is a kitchen and restrooms; they've already got tables and chairs and portable room dividers, and the funeral home is donating gurneys. She paused and grimaced at the implication.

"That was fast work," Barlow said with a broad smile.

"It's extraordinary. Should the hospital wish to expand the clinics to other parts of the city, their timeline of how it was done would be great to replicate."

Barlow gave her a side glance. "Let's not get too ahead of ourselves," he said. "I want to see how this works out first before contemplating another."

"Fair enough."

"We have to provide the staff, too, you know."

"Of course. Do you know if Doctor Browne has determined how that will be done?"

"I thought he might have told you," Barlow said and noticed her hesitation.

"I can certainly ask that, but I think it more appropriate for you."

"Of course. Have you had a look at the building project here this week? They're putting up the interior walls already. Funny about construction: it seems to go so slowly at first and then it gathers steam and soon it will be ready," Barlow said.

"You may have seen the sketches the artist made for the mural on the walls of the reception room. The children will think they are in the midst of a jungle. It will almost be better than going to the zoo. He's hidden all kinds of animals in the bushes and undergrowth. Something for the mothers to talk about with their children."

"A distraction."

"Exactly."

"Thank you, Miss Burnside." The meeting was over, and Amanda was proud of her progress. When she returned to her small office, she was surprised to see Valerie, one of her longtime friends, seated at the other small desk.

"Well, hello!" she said.

"I was feeling a bit guilty about not putting in my hours, so here I am to help," she said, smiling so her dimples showed in her cheeks.

"Let's see, I don't know if there is anything for you to do as I wasn't expecting any help. Why don't you come downstairs with me, and we can look at the progress of the clinic's new building?"

"Gosh," Valerie said, putting on her coat and a warm hat on her short dark hair. "I've been away from here so long I forgot about the renovation."

"Busy with engagement plans?" Amanda asked as they strode to the elevator.

"Actually, Emerson and I have called it off."

Amanda had no response but widened her eyes at the news.

"He quit the job with the architectural firm."

They rode down for a few floors and at the seventh floor two people got in, which silenced their conversation. When they got out on the ground floor, Amanda put her hand on Valerie's arm in sympathy.

"He said he was looking to train as an architect. What changed his mind?"

"I don't know. But I couldn't take this endless changing of jobs and careers. First, he was here at the hospital, then at the financial firm, and now this. My parents had commented on it before, but finally I realized that he would never be a reliable wage earner. How could that make for a stable marriage? Was he expecting my parents to support us? Was he expecting me to go to work? Doing what, exactly? Can you imagine?"

No, Amanda could not. People from their backgrounds did not send their wives out to work. She had already crossed that invisible line with her new job.

"Well, I'm working," she said.

"Because you want to, not because you're married to someone who can't support you."

"That's a shame. Emerson is such a nice fellow," Amanda said.

"Yes. But nice does not pay the bills."

They had gone out the back doors of the hospital and were walking toward the clinic building.

"It reminds me of that character in Bleak House who can't seem to stick with anything and leaves his wife a widow with a child to bring up on her own."

"How sad! Where did you read that?" Valerie asked.

"My father is a Dickens fan and he read a chapter to us each evening after dinner when we were young. Such colorful characters with preposterous names—it was hard keeping them straight. By the end of each chapter, we were nodding off, anyway. Being an attorney himself, my father got a kick out of the nefarious lawyer."

Valerie frowned, never having read the book and not being able to imagine enjoying the antics of a 'nefarious lawyer.'

"See, they haven't changed the dimensions of the building, but they have done miracles with the interior," Amanda said.

Unlike her previous visits where the workmen were outside standing around a fire in an ashcan, they were all inside, a blessing in the cold weather. Amanda shouted out to make someone aware of their presence and was greeted by a different foreman than the one she had interacted with previously.

"Oh, hello. I'm Miss Burnside and this is Miss Mitchell. Where is Joe Greco?"

He shrugged. "I don't know him. I got hired two weeks ago to speed up the process."

Amanda looked around. "It looks like it's coming along nicely. See, Valerie, they've put ceilings in. No more cold drafts floating down from above in the winter or heat coming in through the roof."

"The reception area looks bigger," Valerie said. "Oh, dear, someone has scribbled all over the wall!"

Amanda laughed. "That's what the artist called a cartoon for the mural he will be painting on the wall."

"How modern it will be."

"That's the idea. May we look at some of the rooms?" Amanda asked.

"Sure, help yourself. Be careful of nails on the ground and wet paint," he said.

They could see that the exam rooms had been delineated by walls that reached the new ceiling, an improvement on the former warehouse building that had been converted into the original clinic. There used to be a door at the end of the hall, locked, behind which was storage. Now that the workers had opened that door, Amanda and Valerie could see that the former storage area was enormous and afforded the space to add more exam rooms.

"What a change!" Valerie said, rubbing her gloved hands together for warmth.

"It will be so much better when they get the heat working, however. Let's go back."

They walked quickly past the parking lot and toward the back doors of the hospital when Fred came out and was startled to see them both.

"Oh, hello."

"Hello," Amanda said. There was an awkward silence.

They began talking over one another, Amanda telling him about the clinic's progress while he was explaining that he was going to lunch. They stopped short at the same moment, and Amanda hoped he would not invite them to join him.

"I'm popping home to see my mother. She's been out of town for a bit and if we don't catch up soon, she'll have flown away again." He smiled, tipped his hat and was off to his car.

"I thought you had been stepping out with him," Valerie said.

"Yes, but not anymore."

"What happened?"

"Nothing happened. Maybe that was the problem. It just kind of fizzled."

Valerie turned to look at Fred's retreating form. "He seems like a nice, reliable fellow."

"Yes, he is. Maybe you should make him a closer acquaintance now that you are free."

Valerie looked at her to see if she was joking and saw that was not the case. "Perhaps I shall," she said.

## Chapter 6

Amanda came home to a quiet house. Her father was still at work, but her mother was nowhere to be found. She went to the kitchen where Mary, sitting with the cook having afternoon tea, promptly jumped up at her entrance.

"Sorry, Miss, I was just having a bit of rest."

"That's fine, I was just looking for my mother."

"She went out a short while ago and didn't tell me anything."

"What's that noise?" Amanda said, hearing clacking noises coming from behind the basement door.

The cook and Mary looked at one another but said nothing.

Amanda went closer to the basement door, then opened it and the noise became louder. A few minutes later, she found the source. Nora was seated at a small table in front of a typewriter with her head down in deep concentration.

"Nora!" The girl jumped up and turned a bright red.

"Sorry, Miss. I was just practicing."

To Amanda's puzzled face, she elaborated: "I've been taking a course in business and Cook allowed me a short time to practice."

"You know how to type?"

"Yes, I've learned how and now I am practicing my speed and accuracy."

"That's amazing. I suppose the idea is that you don't wish to be a maid for your entire life."

"Exactly. No offense meant, but a secretary's job pays a lot more. I've even learned shorthand."

"That is impressive. I've seen Miss Bailey at the hospital doing that but thought it much too complicated to attempt." She looked over at the sheet of paper that Nora had been transcribing and smiled. "Have you applied for any jobs yet?"

Nora bit her lip. "Yes, Miss. I was going to tell your mother but not until something certain came along."

"Of course. You wouldn't want to be out of a job before the next one is in place." She hurried to add, "Not that my mother would let you go just because you were trying to better yourself financially."

"Thank you. I'll get back to work upstairs then." Nora scurried past her up the stairs and Amanda looked to see what she had been typing. It was an article from that morning's newspaper where the Mayor had been interviewed and stated that crime was down in the city and the safety of its residents was assured.

Amanda went to Louisa's room to see how she was holding up from the trauma of being sent away and found her not as upset as expected.

"I hope you are not plotting something," she said, observing her sister writing at her desk.

"Not at all. I'm just writing a farewell letter to Rob."

"Farewell for now? Or farewell forever?"

Louisa turned around in her chair. "Obviously not forever. Just giving him the address where I'll be and how to contact me."

"Do be careful. Mother and Daddy have been very patient with you, and you don't want to muck things up. They could make your life infinitely worse if they liked."

Louisa returned to her writing. "Don't be absurd. I intend to look and act heartbroken at being sent away and play on their heartstrings as much as possible."

Amanda sat down on the bed. "Maybe you'll meet somebody else while you're there."

The response was a derisive sniff.

"Okay, so you won't meet an equally handsome, suave nightclub owner. But I'll bet you'll encounter some college men or cadets."

"I have been reading up on Charleston and it sounds charming. At least there are tons of things to do there, old plantations, lots of parties."

"That should keep you occupied for a few days," Amanda said.

Louise folded her letter and put it in an envelope.

"Surely you've told Rob you're going away?"

"Of course. We talk on the phone every day. I'm going to give this to him tonight."

"Louisa, you're getting on an early train tomorrow morning."

"I can sleep on the train. You and I are going to the Oasis tonight so he can bid me farewell."

"Oh, no, you don't," Amanda began.

"Just this one last time, dear sister. And then I'll be out of your hair."

Amanda sighed. "I suppose I could do with a glass of champagne after my day. What's the plan?"

There was no plan as such; Louisa would have dinner with the family and look mopey and tired and excuse herself shortly with the mention of finishing packing and getting to bed early. Sometime after the parents had settled down to reading or gone early to bed themselves, the sisters would sneak down the back stairs and take Amanda's car to the Oasis.

"Just remember, we'll only stay there for an hour at most," Amanda said.

"You're welcome to the loan of a dress," her sister replied.

"Yes, that, too."

THE CLUB DISTRICT was busy even on that weeknight and one would almost guess that Prohibition had ended. But it had not, and the clubs all served drinks in teacups, which was supposed to look as if everyone had coffee rather than the alcoholic brown liquid they consumed. No one was fooled, but neither did anyone get arrested.

The doorman in his outlandish Arabian outfit came to the passenger side of the car and assisted Louisa out, saying, "Good evening, Miss Burnside."

Then he went to the driver's side and took the keys from Amanda with the same greeting. She didn't know if she should be flattered or surprised that he knew her name. If this was to be anything like her previous visit, at least she wouldn't be likely to bump into any of her parents' friends. The clientele was for the most part the young club-hopping type who wanted to be seen in as many top spots as possible in one evening. The other mainstays were politicians and tough-looking men in expensive suits; Amanda hoped these were not gangsters, not that she would know what they were supposed to look like.

It was still early in the evening, which Amanda hoped would mean her sister would get some sleep that night, but the place was filling up quickly with people. Glancing around, she exhaled, seeing that she didn't recognize anyone except the band members, the singer and Rob, who flashed his bright smile at Louisa. He kissed her cheek in greeting and nodded at Amanda.

"I'm heartbroken about the newest developments," he said. "Being in South Carolina will be like being on another planet."

"My friends are very staid," Louisa said. "I don't believe there are any nightclubs in that city." She surveyed the room and made eye contact with Sofia, who was singing a torch song and pretended to ignore the newcomers.

49

Rob laughed. "Trust me, there are clubs anywhere people want them. I couldn't possibly attest to the quality of their beverages, however."

He led them to a table near the front and, as they sat, Sofia turned her attention in the other direction. "I'll be just a minute," he said walking toward the back of the room.

"There's the weasel who sent the flowers," Louisa said, just loud enough that she was sure Sofia could hear her.

"Ah, very clever, indeed," Amanda said. "She has—what—three weeks to make her move?"

"Rob and I will be talking daily. She won't have a chance to get between us."

Amanda wasn't so sure. The woman was very beautiful with her auburn hair, clinging dresses and maturity. Experience went a long way with men, and Amanda was certain that Louisa couldn't hold a candle to her in that department. She looked at her sister, who appeared to be a young woman just out of school infatuated with a man of the world, and wondered where their relationship could ever go.

The waiter came by and delivered two cups of 'coffee,' which turned out to be whisky diluted with a bit of seltzer, a very fine whiskey, indeed. Amanda had hardly put her cup down after the first sip when she heard a voice behind her.

"I see you're becoming a regular," Halloran said.

"As are you," she parried as she turned, having recognized his voice. He was in a dinner jacket, and she suspected it wasn't a rental since it fit him so well.

"Do you find the need to own evening clothes? Or do you moonlight as a gigolo?" Amanda asked.

"Sadly, no. Although I would make quite a bit more money if I did. May I?" he asked as he sat down at their little round table without waiting for a response. "Were you looking for one?"

"Not yet," Amanda said. "Check in with me in about forty years."

Sofia, still singing, turned in their direction to see who had joined them and gave a small smile and wink at Halloran.

"Honestly, that woman," Louisa remarked.

"I would suggest you be nice to that woman," Halloran said.

"Why?"

"She's Morelli's kid sister."

Louisa's eyes widened at the information.

"Changed her name when she went on the stage. Watch out, she could be even nastier than you might imagine."

"Who's Morelli?" Amanda whispered.

"Head of the Italian gang. Don't you read the papers?"

"The newspapers we get at our house don't mention anything about gangs. If you are to believe what you read each day, you'll know from the Mayor's own pronouncement that crime has decreased in the city and he's the one to take credit for it."

Halloran laughed. "Ah, yes, Henry's public relations at work again. I believe the two of them have the editors in their pockets. Besides, who wants to rile up the public with stories of violence, shootings and knifings?"

Amanda gave him a warning glance that was meant to tell him she hadn't shared her day's adventures with the family.

The song was over and followed by polite applause, Sofia bowed and swished her skirts in their direction, moving backstage while the band struck up another number.

"It seems Mr. Worley is doing quite well here," Halloran said, looking around at the crowded tables. "I don't notice his partner José or Caroline." Swiveling his head around, he added, "Nor any of the other high-profile regulars."

"It's early yet," Louisa said.

A waiter approached and asked if he wanted anything, but he shook his head.

"On duty?"

"No, just being abstemious. What is the occasion for you young ladies?" He looked back and forth between the sisters and Louisa lowered her eyes.

"Louisa just needed a little cheering up. All those exams and papers at school have worn her out. She needed a vacation," Amanda said with a straight face.

"What are you studying?" he asked.

"Social work," Louisa answered.

"With an emphasis on the social part," Amanda said.

The band abruptly brought the tune they were playing to an end and Halloran followed their hasty exit, suddenly alert.

"I think you had better gather your things," he said, getting up.

A whistle blew and women in the crowd screamed in alarm. "It's a raid," Halloran said and took Amanda's arm; she in turn grabbed her sister's. He propelled them forward and motioned to the corridor leading backstage. "Hurry. You don't want to be in the newspapers tomorrow."

There was pandemonium in the club, with chairs scraping backwards, men yelling, police blowing their whistles, women screaming and somebody pointlessly telling everyone to remain calm.

Halloran led the Burnside sisters down a narrow corridor past a partially open storeroom, restrooms and then the wide-open dressing room door of Sofia. She sat with her legs crossed, blowing cigarette smoke toward the ceiling as she watched them go by. The band members had gathered in the room with her and appeared nonchalant about the goings on in the main part of the club.

"Why aren't they running out?" Amanda asked.

"They are not the point of this raid is why." He pushed on the door over which an illuminated EXIT sign hung, letting in a cold blast of air.

"What about our wraps?" Louisa asked.

"I'll get them after you're out safely," he said.

No one was outside the back door of the club, and he was able to trot over to the parking lot where there was an unoccupied wooden shed with a board on which hung dozens of car keys. The sisters followed him.

"There's mine," Amanda said, looking over her shoulder, imagining that they were about to be apprehended.

He took down hers and found his and walked them to her car.

"I don't understand—what's the point of this raid?"

"To put the frights into Rob Worley."

"He doesn't frighten easily," Louisa said.

"No, but the loss of revenue might bother him. It's all about the money. There goes tonight's take. And people may stay away for a few nights longer, although they don't usually raid the same place twice in a row," he said rubbing his thumb against his fingers in the time-old gesture indicating a bribe. "Protection. So, it doesn't happen again."

"The gang or the police?"

He shrugged. "I'm not with the vice squad, but either one is possible."

The sisters looked at each other with surprise.

"It's been quite a day for seeing and learning new things," Amanda said. "And few of them pleasant." She opened the driver's side door, reached over and popped the lock for Louisa's door. "Thank you for the rescue. But we don't have our wraps."

"At your service, Miss." He left them with the engine running while he went back inside and a few minutes later came out with their coats and handed them in to the grateful sisters. They drove out the back exit of the parking lot, not wanting to encounter a paddy wagon that might be out front, likely surrounded by photographers.

But it was a low-key event that evening, with one small van in the event anyone got unruly. All the customers were pushing and shoving their way out the front doors, hastily putting their coats on and keeping their heads down. The doorman leaned against the building with his arms crossed over his beaded vest, took off his turban with the phony jewel to scratch his head and waited for the turmoil to settle.

Halloran's previous entry to retrieve the wraps had gone unnoticed. This time he went back through the front doors as if he had just arrived and saw several cops roaming around the room, picking up teacups and sniffing, some drinking the dregs while Rob Worley looked on helplessly.

## Chapter 7

Because Louisa had to get up before dawn to catch an early train, everyone in the family had to get up, along with Cook coming in to supply them with a hot breakfast. As it turned out, Mr. Burnside could have booked a ticket on a later train and only purchased the earlier one to make sure that Louisa wouldn't be out late the night before. Little did they know she had tricked them again and returned early enough that, when they peeked into her bedroom at ten o'clock, they assumed she was fast asleep.

"See, Edward, your words struck a chord with her, and she has decided to behave herself," her mother had said.

"Hmph," he had responded. "I'm almost tempted to prod that lump under the covers to make sure she hasn't piled pillows there to deceive us. And don't tell me you weren't worried that she might run away with that scoundrel."

Over the six months since they had first learned of Rob Worley, their opinion of him had begun by thinking of him as a low life but then changed when he showed up at the beach house in Maine, with his impeccable manners and gracious assistance in a deadly situation. After that, they had thought better of him. Partly that was because he was going back to Boston and Louisa remained with them. Recently, having learned that she was seeing him on a regular basis, they had revised their assessment and thought him a great threat to their daughter's reputation. It also smarted that she had used every sort of subterfuge to see him, including pretending to enroll in college classes and using the money her father supplied for tuition and books on evening gowns to wear to Worley's nightclub. They had never been to a nightclub in their lives, but they were certain it was a seedy environment with disreputable characters. Not their class at all.

Amanda stumbled down to the breakfast room in her nightclothes and robe, an unusual occurrence as the family habitually took their first meal of the day fully dressed. But it was still dark out, she was sleepy and tired of Louisa's antics and her part in covering for her sister. Nightgown and robe would do. She was a bit surprised that her mother seemed to have taken the same attitude and was similarly attired. Her father had on a three-piece suit to take his younger daughter to the train station, in part not trusting that she would get on the train until he actually saw her in the car with her luggage loaded.

"Where is she?" Margaret asked. There was still a niggle of worry that Louisa would do something to impede her departure.

True to form, Louisa made a dramatic appearance shortly thereafter, dressed all in black.

Amanda rolled her eyes and dug into the pancakes that Cook had made specially to fortify the younger child for the long journey. She was only going to New York to spend the day at her aunt and uncle's home in Pelham, hardly an arduous trip, then on to Charleston the next day.

Little was said as they ate until Mrs. Burnside thought that some last-minute instructions were necessary.

"Now, Louisa, you are to write us every other day about what you are doing, and we expect a Sunday night telephone call from you."

"Yes, Mother," she said, trying to look as if she were going to her own funeral.

"And I want you to cease communications with Mr. Worley," Mr. Burnside said.

Louisa looked up abruptly.

"Entirely. You are nineteen years old. He is much older and experienced, no doubt. We do not want you sullying your reputation by associating with him any longer."

Louisa didn't meet his gaze but continued eating.

"Am I clear?"

"Yes, Daddy. Perfectly."

Amanda considered the conversation one-sided. Her father had made his demands and Louisa acknowledged them, but she never said she agreed to the terms. This Southern vacation would only hold off the inevitable, Amanda thought.

Mr. Burnside checked his watch. "We'd better be going. Is your luggage downstairs already?"

"Yes, Daddy. I just need to get my coat and we can leave."

He bustled about getting his own hat, coat and gloves before retrieving his car and bringing it round to the front of the house.

After all the threats and recriminations, Mrs. Burnside weepily bade her younger daughter farewell. Amanda gave her a hug and muttered something in her ear while she looked forward to her own departure back to bed.

They stood at the front door and waved as the pair drove off down the street, Mrs. Burnside and Amanda shivering as they returned to the sitting room.

"This respite will be good for us all," Amanda said, thinking of not having to create alibis for her sister for a few weeks. Her mother didn't want to admit it, but she was also relieved. For the time being.

"You know The Citadel is in Charleston. Maybe Louisa will meet some rich, handsome Southern cadet," Amanda added.

"One thing at a time, dear," her mother answered wearily as they both went upstairs.

INTERVIEWING the parents of a dead child, no matter what age, was a task that no policeman enjoyed and being no different, Halloran and Dominic dragged their feet getting to the Rinaldis' house. They looked at the list of names and apartment numbers and, rather than ringing the bell in the entrance which might draw the attention of the other residents, then trudged their way up to the fourth floor through the dingy hallways, ill-lit by low wattage light bulbs.

There was a hesitation at their knock and the door opened a crack with a brown eye taking in who it was. Mr. Rinaldi opened the door fully and bade them come in. He was fully dressed for the day in a suit and tie. The apartment was warm and still smelled of a recent meal that involved garlic and strong coffee.

"May I get you coffee?"

"No, no," Halloran said, removing his hat. "We wanted to express our condolences and see if there is any other information we should know about Giovanni that can help us find who did this."

Mr. Rinaldi shook his head.

"I think we need to include your wife in the conversation."

"She is not well. Her nerves…."

"I understand, but she might be able to tell us something important."

The man hesitated, then reluctantly went down the hall and entered what must have been their bedroom. The detectives glanced around the room in which they stood and took in the substantial furniture and the prominent portrait of Jesus revealing his sacred heart. A white rosette hung from a ribbon across one corner of the painting, likely a remnant of someone's confirmation.

Mr. Rinaldi returned a few minutes later holding his wife by the elbow. The detectives stood up. Her eyes were swollen, and she staggered as she walked to one of the chairs facing the sofa and they sat on the sofa opposite.

"Again, our condolences. Mrs. Rinaldi. We need to ask you if your son was at all agitated yesterday before he went to work?"

"No," she said with some surprise, clutching a hand-kerchief.

"Was anything preying on his mind recently? Did he mention any difficulty with anybody? Arguments or fights?"

She looked at her husband. "No. He seemed fine. He doesn't fight with people."

"Was he involved in a gang?"

"No!" Rinaldi said with emphasis. "He's a good boy. He works at the store. Sometimes he visits some friend up the alley. Some boy named Mario?" He looked at his wife for confirmation but she shrugged.

"What do you think happened?"

"Someone tried to rob him, that's what happened," she said, holding the handkerchief up to her mouth.

"No money was gone," her husband corrected her. "Nothing was stolen."

"Then why did they do this to him?" She collapsed against her husband's shoulder and heaved with sobs.

"We know who did it," Rinaldi said with a scowl.

"Who?"

The man clamped his mouth shut and would not say anything more.

"We'll do our best to find out what happened. If you can think of anyone who wanted to hurt him or anything else we should know, please call us." Halloran dug into his pocket and pulled out a card with his name and the police station's number on it and handed it to the father.

They went down the stairs, noticing that some doors were discreetly opened to watch their passing. As they got to the first floor, they heard a hissing sound and realized that someone from behind the door of one of the apartments was trying to get their attention. They approached a middle-aged woman who peered over their shoulders to make sure no one else was within earshot. She beckoned them in and shut the door quietly behind them.

"You know what was going on?" she said. She wore an apron over her dress and was wiping her hands on a kitchen towel. Not waiting for an answer, she continued. "The daughter was going out with someone they didn't like. A Sicilian. He and the brother argued about it. Hah— the whole family argued about it, from what I could hear. Ask anyone in the building. With connections like he had, I bet you gangsters are involved."

"Are you Sicilian?" Halloran asked.

Her eyes narrowed. "Of course not. I'm from Rome. The boyfriend's name is Marco Santoro, and he works down at the docks."

"How do you know this?"

"I've got eyes and ears," she said, opening the door and almost shoving them into the hallway. The door closed quietly behind them.

"Now we've got to find the boyfriend," Halloran said.

"Sometimes I really hate this job," Dominic said.

GETTING UP TWO HOURS LATER, Amanda awoke disoriented and for a moment thought it might be the weekend. But no, she was due in at the hospital that morning to go with Fred and the resident to check out the clinic. It was an overcast day, impossible to know where the sun was in the sky, if indeed there was one, and she thought of Louisa's grand adventure in sunny Charleston. Why hadn't she thought to misbehave and be sent away? The reason was it was too much trouble to scheme against her parents and she had yet to meet the man who might urge her to do so.

She was pleasantly surprised to see Valerie had turned up for volunteer duty again at work, even if she was rather slow at processing the paperwork.

"Good morning," Valerie said cheerfully. "We'll get a lot done today seeing as it's the two of us."

"I'll be leaving soon with Fred and one of the staff to have them look at the clinic. I expect we'll be back before lunch."

Fred got held up with some emergency case and they didn't set off until closer to eleven. His angular face was in a scowl as they left, she leading the way in her car and he, with the resident, in his own car following. When they arrived and walked into the building, she asked the janitor if it were an inconvenient time, but he gruffly said it was not. After climbing the steps and looking at the ostentatious building, Fred appeared displeased by the lush furnishings of the first floor and the stage at one end.

"What is this, a ballroom?"

"The clinic will be downstairs," she replied and took them down the stairs to the basement that was set up as a reception area at one end with the portable room dividers stacked against the wall at the other.

"This is more like it," Fred said. "Oh, by the way, this is Doctor Wilkinson," he said, introducing Amanda to the young resident with him. He surveyed the kitchen off to the left that had a wide opening to serve food. "Good. We can set up any testing equipment in there. Restrooms, good. I've got to say this is coming along nicely, Amanda."

She winced at his condescending tone.

"The gurneys are due sometime tomorrow. We've got the room on Tuesday and Wednesday each week. One thing to remember is that it's used for other purposes so that when the last day of the clinic is over, you all will have to restack the dividers and take any equipment with you. All that should be left here are the gurneys, the dividers and the chairs. The janitor will rearrange them as needed for whatever other activities take place here."

"I'm concerned that someone will take the dividers and the gurneys," Fred said.

"Do you think so?" Amanda asked.

"Of course. One thing I've learned at the hospital is that if something isn't nailed down, it quickly grows legs and disappears. They should provide us with a secure place to store them."

"All right then, I'll ask about that. What do you think about the facilities?"

"They'll do," Fred said.

The resident walked into the kitchen to see what was there.

"Is something troubling you?" Amanda asked Fred.

"No, why do you ask?"

"You seem abrupt this morning."

He looked at her. "A medical emergency ate up almost two hours of my morning, meaning I'll have to work late to finish up the paperwork. And I don't appreciate it that you told someone that we weren't seeing each other anymore."

Amanda felt her face turn red. "Who?"

"It doesn't matter. I just don't appreciate it."

"So noted," she replied.

He looked at his watch. "I'd better be getting back." He beckoned to the resident, who thanked her for the tour, walked swiftly to the stairwell and mounted the steps two at a time.

IT DIDN'T TAKE LONG to locate where Marco Santoro worked at the docks. A ship had come in and cranes were being used to unload the cargo onto the dock while men who stood there guided it carefully to the ground. Another set of men were wheeling the crates into a large warehouse, and those workmen, all big, sturdy men, stacked them near the open doors awaiting trucks that would take them away. It was dangerous work, requiring strength and agility in case something shook loose or ropes broke, sending hundreds of pounds hurtling to the ground. It necessitated being alert at all times, even if there was a foreman who was spotting from a perch.

Dominic approached the foreman's aerie and called up to him, but the noise of the winches, the shouting of the men and the sounding of a horn from the ship drowned out the words. Instead, the foreman came down from his high chair and, annoyed, asked what was going on.

Then he added before hearing an answer, "Hey, we don't need civilians wandering around where they could get flattened by something."

Dominic pulled his overcoat open and showed him his badge and explained that he was looking for Marco. The response was a jerk of the thumb in the direction of the warehouse. The two detectives went through the wide doors, looked around and, singling out one man who was not lifting or moving anything as the person in charge, they asked for Marco again.

He looked with disdain at Dominic until he was shown the badge and pointed to someone whose back was turned to them.

"Marco Santoro?" Dominic called out as they approached.

The young man turned with an inquisitive look before realizing that these were strangers and his body tensed as if to flee. But Halloran blocked the move while Dominic went closer.

"We just need to talk to you about the death of Giovanni Rinaldi."

His dark eyes grew wide, and he said, "Yeah, I heard about that. I don't know anything about it."

"Where were you midmorning yesterday?"

"Here," he said, holding his hands out and adding, "where else would I be?"

"What time did you come to work?"

"The usual, five a.m. Ship came in the night before and we had to off-load it. Ask the boss there," he gestured in the direction of the man who had pointed him out.

"Do you guys punch a clock?"

"What do you mean?"

"Who knows when you come in or if you come and go during the day?"

"Are you crazy? We don't get to come and go. We get here before dawn and work hard, half an hour for lunch and knock off early in the afternoon."

"There some problem?" the foreman said, coming over to the conversation.

"No, just checking on his whereabouts yesterday morning."

"Here at the same time as the rest of them. Before dawn. A workingman's day," he said with a sneer, taking in the suits under their overcoats and the polished shoes.

"Get back to work," he said to Marco. "And you guys, beat it."

They took the hint and left, knowing they wouldn't get anything more out of anyone.

"If he was here, he isn't our man," Dominic said.

"I doubt the entire workforce here would lie for him. I'm more surprised that he knew about the murder."

"Nah, word travels fast in the neighborhood."

"I wonder where he lives," Halloran said. "Why don't you go back in and ask him?"

Dominic looked incredulous but went back in, giving the foreman wide berth, and emerged a few minutes later.

"Around here, like most of the stevedores. He told me the address of his mother's apartment."

"Let's go," Halloran said.

It was well known as a rough neighborhood because of the tough men who lived there and brawled as a form of recreation after a long week's work. They found the address Marco had given, a walk-up, probably cold-water apartment, and mounted the stairs to his mother's place.

She opened the door hesitantly and said, "What do you want?"

Halloran showed his badge. "Just a few words. We don't have to come in."

"Good, stay outside. She came out, closed the door behind her and folded her arms across her chest.

"Giovanni Rinaldi was killed yesterday."

"I heard."

"Who told you?"

"I can't remember." She stared straight at Halloran, her black eyes drilling into his.

"Where were you yesterday morning?"

"Me? Here, where do you think? That Giovanni was a hot head. He probably got into a fight with somebody."

"Do you think he got into a fight with your son?"

"No! How could he? Marco was at work."

"Where were you?"

"Me? I was here. Sleeping. I work the night shift."

"Where?"

"Argento's factory down the street."

Halloran looked at Dominic.

"The sausage factory," he said.

She glared at them. "I work on the line. Cutting up the meat as it goes by."

"Can anyone vouch for you?"

"What do you mean?"

"That you were here shortly before midday?"

"Of course not. My son is at work, I get my sleep during the day. What do you think, I go prowling around looking for some kid who kept trying to pick a fight with my son? Yeah, I bet the family didn't mention anything about the threats, did they? 'Leave my sister alone.' Yelling out in the street up at the apartment. Go ahead, ask anybody in the building." Her voice had become louder as she went on, and one of the neighbor's heads looked down from the floor above to see what the noise was about.

"Yeah, you. You probably heard him yelling out in the street!"

The head disappeared quickly, and Mrs. Santoro breathed heavily.

"Does anybody else live here?" Halloran asked.

"Like who?"

"Like a Mr. Santoro?"

She snorted. "Long gone. The bum. And good riddance to him. Why do you think I've got to work? Not enough money from Marco's job to keep the both of us. With this landlord who threatens to raise the rent even more? And who's going to want to rent a dump like this in this neighborhood?"

Halloran felt she could probably go on for another thirty minutes with her list of grievances, so he decided to cut the discussion short. If they needed to talk to her again, they could do so.

"Okay, okay," he said holding his hands up in surrender. "That's all for now."

"For now? You better not come back. There's nothing more to tell." She put her chin up aggressively, pushed the door open and slammed it behind her.

"Phew," Halloran said as they descended the stairway, veering around a baby carriage that sat outside a door.

"She went easy on you. I heard that when her husband left, she chased him down the street with a knife."

AFTER FRED LEFT, Amanda was peeved, never having experienced that mood from him before. She put her gloves back on and followed him, one step at a time, up to the first floor and then out onto the street. She didn't walk straight to her car but went to look at some of the shops on the other side of the street that she had not seen before. Perhaps she could locate that restaurant that Fred had introduced her to last year before they were seriously dating. Then she thought perhaps that was the reason Fred was out of sorts, remembering that pleasant evening. She hadn't taken their dating as the prelude to marriage and realized that he it was precisely how he had seen it.

The wind had picked up and the sky was still leaden, so she pulled the collar up around her neck and stayed close to buildings as she walked. A pharmacy with a mortar and pestle ornament hanging from a rod over the front door was next to a door indicating a dentist had his offices upstairs. She craned her neck to see that almost every shop had a tenant on the second floor, some of them professionals, and others, without nameplates, might be the living quarters for the retailers below. When she came to the corner, there was a flimsy, three-sided wooden structure with magazines, newspapers, cigarettes and candy for sale. She said hello to the man who stood behind the shallow counter while she looked everything over.

"What kind of candy is that?" she asked.

He shrugged and pointed to the cover of the tin. "Torrone," he said, reading the label as if it were self-explanatory.

"Yes, I see that, but what kind of confection is it? Chocolate? Taffy?"

"It's nougat. Very sweet. With almonds."

"Sounds delicious. I'll take that small one." She looked around at the newspapers, some of which were in Italian, and picked up one with a photo of Mussolini on the front page. "I'll take this, too."

He shook his head. "Can you read Italian?"

"No, but I'll find someone to translate for me."

"I wouldn't buy that if I were you," he said, jutting out his chin.

"But I want to. Here," she dug for her coin purse in her handbag.

He looked over her shoulder to someone standing behind her and she turned. "Oh, Dominic. Fancy meeting you here."

"Sell her the paper, I'll explain everything," he said.

Puzzled by the exchange, she handed over the coins to the man, and Dominic took the paper and folded it so the front photo was obscured, put it under his arm and took her by the arm.

"Come on, I'm meeting Brendan for lunch. You look like you could use a good meal."

She looked at him in surprise. Did he mean that she was too thin? Or that she needed to have some Italian cooking?

They walked another block and she saw that he was leading her to the very restaurant where she had eaten previously, Catalano's. Dominic opened the door for her and even in the little anteroom the delicious smells were in the air.

Halloran was seated at a table facing the door and stood up abruptly. "Well, well."

"I'm glad to see you, too," she said.

He pulled a chair out for her while she hung her coat up on the rack near the door. The two men kept their coats on.

"Are you staying for lunch or about to go out again?"

"We've been out most of the morning and, frankly, most of me is frozen. I need to warm up before I take this coat off."

"Ditto," Dominic said.

"Have you found out what happened to that poor young man?"

"Which one?" Dominic asked.

"The one who worked in the religious shop."

"Not yet. It's complicated," Halloran responded tersely.

"By what?"

He gave a short laugh. "By everything."

A young woman came to the table, bringing them water and smiling at them. "Good afternoon," she said. She handed them menus printed on large cards.

"What's for lunch today?" Dominic asked.

"Mama's made lentil soup with sausage and there's wedding soup. Also, spaghetti with clam sauce and farfalle with capers."

"I'd like a bowl of lentil soup, please, and something hot to drink," Amanda said.

"Coffee?"

"Yes, please."

The men each ordered a cup of soup, pasta and coffee. The waitress disappeared into the kitchen and through the eye-level pass-through the owner's wife, who was also the chef, nodded her head at them.

"What do you mean 'everything,' Detective Halloran?"

"We're having a social lunch. I can be Brendan."

"Please explain, Brendan."

"It's rare when there is an unexplained murder, yet the family *knows* who is responsible. Whether it was the evil eye cast upon them or someone who has it out for the family. If we can get them talking, I bet they will rattle off a handful of suspects."

"Was he so disliked?"

Dominic suppressed a laugh. "No, it's just how things are. Someone was jealous of him. Someone was jealous of the family's good fortune. He looked at a young girl the wrong way and the brother came after him. His family was from Calabria and they're from Apulia. And let's not even get into the politics involved."

"The Mayor's aide made is sound like everyone here is a Democrat," she said.

"I'm talking about the politics back in the Old Country." Dominic pulled the newspaper out from under his arm and discreetly showed it to Halloran as there were other diners in the room.

"What were you doing with this?" he asked him.

"It's mine. I thought the photo was interesting and I was going to ask someone to translate the article," Amanda said.

"No. You do not want to go flashing this around. If you do, you're in one camp and not in the other. Your job here is to get the clinic up and running, not to take sides in the current political tussle," Brendan said.

"I know what my job is, thank you," she said. "I just was curious about international affairs and wanted to get a better feel for the people here."

"Do that by eating their food. Politics should be off the table," he responded.

"It's complicated," Dominic began. "There are regional political affiliations that come into play. And for some years now the fascists have taken control. Some people like the changes, some people don't. And speaking as an Italian, I can say we all have strong opinions when it comes to politics."

"What has that got to do with the man who was killed?"

"Maybe something, maybe nothing. Everybody is talking but nobody is saying anything of use to us."

She sighed, realizing that she would never grasp the nuances of this community.

The waitress came back with the soup, a basket of bread and coffee for them all.

"I hope this is not espresso," Amanda whispered to the men. "Henry introduced me to it."

"It's the only way he can get a woman's pulse to race," Dominic replied. That got a chuckle out of his companion.

"How is the clinic project coming along?" Brendan asked.

"Very well. Fred brought a resident with him this morning to look at the facilities."

"How is Fred?" he asked.

"Very well." She took a spoonful of soup. "This is wonderful for a cold day." She let a few moments go by before adding, "Actually we're not seeing one another anymore." She looked down at her soup and didn't see Dominic glance quickly over to Halloran. They continued to eat in silence until the owner stopped by their table.

"Are you enjoying the soup?"

"It's great," Halloran said. "I see business is good. You even have a waitress now."

"That's my daughter, Simona. She just finished high school and is looking for a job that pays more than her mother's cooking."

"I'll keep an eye out for anything in the Police Department," Halloran said.

"Thank you, Detective. But with apologies, I don't think her mother would like her working where there are bad people."

"We're not bad people," Dominic said with a laugh.

The owner became flustered. "No, no. I mean where bad people come and go. The criminals."

Halloran said. "It's fine, I understand. Some women don't seem to mind, however."

Amanda pretended not to hear that remark; instead, she complimented the owner on the soup. Fortified against the cold after the hearty meal, Amanda was escorted back to her car by Halloran and Dominic, and they continued to the alley where the murder had happened.

"Are you going to ask her out?" Dominic inquired.

"Who?"

"Come on. She practically told you she was available."

Ignoring the comment, he responded, "I want to talk to Giovanni's parents in more detail tomorrow. I know they probably have all kinds of theories about who did it and why, but I think we need to draw them out more."

## Chapter 8

The next day, a telegram from the Burnsides in Pelham, New York, let the family in Beacon Hill know that Louisa had been safely put onto a train to Charleston and would be arriving later that evening.

"And it is a nonstop train, so there is no chance of her changing her mind," Mr. Burnside announced at the breakfast table.

"It's not as if she knows anybody between here and Charleston," Amanda said.

"I'm sure she'll be fine and behave herself. After all, Eunice's mother and aunt are with her as chaperones," Mrs. Burnside said.

Amanda thought her mother was being overly optimistic about what oversight would be employed. After all, Louisa had managed to elude supervision in her own home.

"What are your plans for today, Amanda?" her mother asked.

"I'm meeting the girls for our monthly luncheon."

"How nice that you have kept in touch with your friends."

"It's thanks to Valerie, who declared that we needed to stick together and arranged for her club to host us, that the tradition continues. We're down to about ten since Doris and Ava got married and left town, one to Providence and the other to Hingham."

Mr. Burnside chuckled. "Hingham is hardly out of town."

"With a new baby she can't spend most of a day getting here and back," Amanda said.

Her parents were quiet, and she knew that any mention of her friends who were married or had a child put them in the mood to focus on her single state. She changed the subject quickly.

"Besides, I'm dying to hear about the cruise that Patricia went on."

"I hope you're not thinking of lobbying for a cruise now that Louisa managed to get a trip to Charleston out of us," her father said.

"Not at all. I've got a job, remember? I can't just go traipsing around. I'm just curious about her experience."

"Don't eat too much at lunch, dear. Cook is making a nice roast for dinner," her mother said.

"Not a chance. I heard one of the waiters refer to our lunches as 'rabbit food,' if that gives you any indication. Light salads—nothing heavy. Marnie insists."

"She's already very trim. Surely, she's not trying to lose weight?" her mother asked.

"She has a part-time job as a model for Monsieur Dubois' salon and they seem to want their girls to be thin as rails."

SHE GOT to the club at twelve-thirty and realized she was only the second one there.

"Did I mistake the time?" she asked Cecile, who was patting the back of her hair into shape.

"Don't be daft. Everyone thinks it's fashionable to be late." She took out a cigarette case and offered one to Amanda, who shook her head.

She was becoming annoyed that she was the only one with an actual job who needed to be somewhere after the meal while the others could swan in, take their places leisurely and stay as long as they liked.

"Oh, don't be so cross. Everyone will think that you consider yourself superior because you're concerned about indigent children." She exhaled the smoke. "Not that you aren't, but work is not something that interests me. That's for the menfolk to take on."

"That's certainly the mainstream opinion."

"Why change the natural order of things? I'd be happy to keep a home, continue to play bridge and volunteer on some committee or other to do with the arts. That will be enough for me."

"Children?"

"Not if I can help it. Perhaps if a nanny is involved."

Amanda was surprised her friend had her specific future mapped out. "And who is the lucky man?" she asked with a smile.

"Working on it. I've been seeing two very suitable choices. Stay tuned, as the radio announcers say."

Betsy and Valerie came in, arm in arm, and greeted their friends, followed shortly by Gayle, flustered by being late. They took their seats and sipped white grape juice waiting for the others.

"For a moment, I thought we might be having white wine," Cecile said. "Alas, no."

"It's not that kind of place," Valerie said, put out that Cecile would cast aspersions on her club, which was one of the toniest in Boston.

"Hi, hi," sang out Patricia, sailing through the doorway, and everyone gasped at her tan and her much blonder hair.

"Is that natural?" Betsy asked.

"Of course. Three weeks sailing around in the sunshine didn't just lighten my mood." She sat down and smiled around the table.

"Sunshine?" someone said. "What's that?"

"I heard Louisa is joining Eunice in South Carolina," Betsy said.

"Yes, she managed to squeeze a trip south from my father."

"Lucky duck."

"I'll say," Amanda said.

"I thought she was going to school. It's not Easter vacation for some time yet."

"True, but she lost interest in her studies," Amanda said. She was glad that nobody there seemed to know the real reasons.

"What was she studying?"

"Social work."

Gayle grimaced. "Does that mean wandering around in the slums doing good deeds?"

"Doesn't anyone want to hear about my trip?" Patricia pouted.

"Not really," Betsy said. "It makes me green with envy that you got to go."

"Did you meet any millionaires?" Gayle asked.

"Of course! Who else could afford to be gone in the middle of winter for three weeks?"

"I imagine broke fortune hunters might find the time," Cecile said.

"There were some of those, that's for sure."

"Do tell!" Gayle said.

"There was the most charming Cuban fellow. Tall, dark and handsome with the most charming accent."

Several of the girls cooed over the notion. "Like Cary Grant?"

"Wrong accent and handsomer. The first night out of Miami he told us that his father had died, and he was going home to his family's sugar plantation to salvage their fortune."

"And…?"

"And I thought he would. When we got to Havana, he got off the ship and that was the last we saw of him. Until…." She took a sip of her juice waiting for the reaction of the group.

"Until what?"

"Until bouquets of flowers were delivered to our hotel room the next day and he appeared the day after that."

"How romantic!" Betsy said.

"Yes, I thought so, too. But my mother was wise enough to ask around and found out that while he had the right family name, he was not the son of the plantation owner, but the nephew, looking for a rich American woman to marry. Such is life."

"Maybe you could have supported him. It's not like you're lining up at a soup kitchen every day," Cecile said.

"No, but if he were so extravagant about the flowers, I imagine he would be a spendthrift in other ways." She lowered her voice to a whisper. "And those Latin men are womanizers, as everyone knows."

The waiters came in with trays of the meager entrees and on their heels Marnie arrived breathless. "Sorry, girls, I got caught in traffic. I'm glad you started without me."

"You never eat anything anyway."

"What were you talking about?"

"Bounders," someone said.

"Fortune hunters," said someone else.

Veronica breezed in just in time for the main dish.

"Forgive me. I was on the phone with Tex."

More than one person said, "Who?"

"Oops, forgot to tell you. I met the dreamiest cowboy at the dude ranch in Scottsdale."

"What did your mother say?"

"She was too busy paying attention to the owner!" She laughed and they all joined in.

"But, back to reality now."

"Sounds wonderful," Marnie said. "Amanda! I heard you have an actual job! What are you doing?"

"I'm working for the director of Mercy Hospital trying to get clinic locations in other parts of the city."

"How exciting! Such as where?"

"Right now we're about to open a site in the North End."

The room went quiet.

"Isn't that kind of a rough area?" Gayle asked.

"No, not really," Amanda said, ignoring the recent murder and focusing on more positive aspects. "It's very lively, lots of people on the street, every kind of shop and store you can imagine, bustling all the time. And the food is extraordinary."

"What do you mean?"

"It's foreign to our bland tastes but very good. Wonderful bread and a heavy use of garlic."

"Sounds delicious, but I couldn't have garlic on my breath and show up at the salon," Marnie said.

"You don't eat anything anyhow. All you care about is fitting into those slinky dresses," Amanda said.

"Isn't Italian food a fattening type of diet?" Betsy asked.

"Not really. Everything in moderation, right?"

"I think it's very odd that a portion of the city with our significant historic sites like the North Church and Paul Revere's house should be where immigrants now live," Betsy said.

"You could always move back there," Cecile commented.

"No thank you. I like the calm of Brookline, the trees and the lack of bustling streets."

"Oh, aren't we such snobs?" They all laughed.

"I heard you are seeing Fred Browne," Veronica said to Valerie, who blushed deeply and looked down at her plate.

Amanda smiled slightly to cover her surprise.

"Yes, we went for a lovely meal at some obscure French restaurant. It was charming."

Amanda knew exactly which one that was. The place where he had first broached the topic of engagement to her. He must be anxious to tie the knot with someone to have moved on so quickly.

"I want to hear all about Cuba," Valerie said, turning the conversation away from herself.

"It was marvelous. Warm breezes, delightful beaches, fresh fish, rum!"

"Did your mother let you drink?"

"Of course—she was looking for a partner in crime since my father wasn't along for the trip."

The room erupted in laughter.

"Oh, don't worry, you can get that here in Boston if you know the right people," Amanda said.

All heads turned in her direction.

"Thus spake Miss Goody Two Shoes," Cecile said, lighting up a cigarette.

"I don't spend all my time tending to the needs of the impoverished, you know."

"Do tell."

"In the course of my work, I've had the experience of visiting a few nightclubs and a speakeasy."

"Aren't they the same thing?" Gayle asked.

"Nightclubs have entertainment and food. Speakeasies serve the hard stuff."

"Did you go by yourself?"

"Of course not. I was accompanied by a charming companion."

"Who?"

Amanda realized she had dug a nice hole for herself but didn't want to be too cagey lest her friends think she was going out with a gangster. She dropped the bomb. "A handsome police detective."

$\sim$

HALLORAN AND DOMINIC first went to the shop to see if it was open, but the shades were down, and the broken back window was covered with plywood. Peering through the glass of an intact window they could see that the damaged statues had been swept away.

They walked down the quiet alley toward the building at the end, which was multistory apartments. In the entryway, Halloran rang the bell to the Rinaldis' while Dominic stood outside waiting for Mr. Rinaldi's head to poke out a window and beckon them inside.

They made their way slowly up to the fourth floor and knocked on the Rinaldis' door, which the father quickly opened. He motioned them back to the sofa they had sat on the previous day, once again asked if they would like coffee. They removed their hats and declined the offer, asking instead if his wife was able to talk with them, too. He closed his eyes slowly and said he would find out. He was gone a few minutes and they could hear murmuring from a room down the hall.

A door opened and three people came down the hall: the father, the mother and a young girl who was introduced as Giovanni's sister, Angela. Halloran and Dominic stood and solemnly shook hands with the newcomers before everyone sat down, the family pulling chairs to face the detectives.

"I'm sorry we have to talk to you again, but we need more information."

The mother bit her lip then the words burst out of her. "I don't know why you come asking the same questions. We told you already. We know who did this and why. Why haven't you arrested Santoro yet?"

Halloran saw the young girl tense up at the mention of the name.

"We've questioned him already and he was nowhere near the shop when Giovanni was attacked."

"Who says? Sure, he'd make up a lie. Like he lies about everything else. We told him to stay away from Angela, but he wouldn't listen. That's why he killed Giovanni." She began to cry and pulled a crumpled handkerchief out of her pocket and wiped her eyes roughly.

Halloran knew that the parents disapproved of the boy Angela was seeing but their insistence that he committed the murder didn't make it so. Although it was no use arguing with them about that point. They were stuck on that explanation and were not going to let go of it.

"Can you think of any reason why the statues were destroyed? At first, we thought that perhaps there was a prolonged fight, but there was no plaster dust on his body. It seems the broken statues were broken after the attack."

Mr. Rinaldi shook his head. "No, why would anyone do that? It's senseless."

"Was there anyone you didn't recognize from the neighborhood come into the shop in the days before?" Dominic asked.

"No. This is a slow time of year. It picks up in Lent, then Easter and First Communion in May. Just women from the neighborhood, some I don't know their names. No rough-looking men."

Halloran stopped for a moment and realized that everyone had assumed it must have been a big man who crashed around the shop and then knifed Giovanni. Or knifed him and then smashed the statues. But it could have been a woman. A woman with a grudge who broke the statues out of revenge. A jilted girlfriend? An over-protective mother?

Angela got up abruptly. "I'll go get the bread for lunch," she said, moving to the coatrack in the corner and dressing for the cold weather. Her parents said nothing as she left the apartment.

"Can you think of anyone else who would wish your son harm? Or anyone who wanted to destroy your business?"

Clearly the latter question had not occurred to Mr. Rinaldi before this, and Halloran almost regretted that he had asked it since they would now have to hear of all the people who were jealous of the family's success or a rival in the religious artifact business.

He looked at his wife who searched her brain for a name but could not come up with anything other than the detested boyfriend.

"Was your son seeing anybody?"

That baffled the parents, who didn't understand what that meant.

"I mean, was he going out with a girl?"

The father stood up. "No! He was a good boy!" He sat down again, as if surprised at the strength of his own reaction.

Almost a minute went by as Halloran observed the uneasiness of the two seated facing them. Then he got up, thanked them for their time and said that the body would be released to the funeral home in the next few days so they could prepare for the funeral.

They left, plopping their hats back on their heads before emerging from the entryway and into the wind whipping around the corner. As they approached the side street that led out to Hanover, they saw Angela coming back with a loaf of bread sticking out of a paper bag. She stopped when she saw them.

"It's not Marco who did this. I know it. You need to look elsewhere. Probably no further than this alley." She didn't wait for a response or say anything else but walked back to the end of the street and turned left toward home.

# Chapter 9

That next day, Mr. Barlow informed her about the date for the ribbon cutting for the new clinic.

"That's moving quickly," she said.

"That Salvatore De Luca is anxious to get it going. It will be Saturday with a lot of fanfare. I hope you can attend."

"I wouldn't miss it for the world," she said.

"Would you like to go, too?" Amanda asked Miss Bailey, who was seated at her desk outside Mr. Barlow's office.

"Do you think I should?"

"I think you would find it very interesting. Knowing what I know now, there will likely be lots of people and certainly lots of food."

"In that case…," she smiled.

"We can go together," Amanda suggested, thinking she would feel more comfortable with a companion in a sea of people she didn't know.

There was an awkward moment when she got back to her office and saw Valerie, who almost didn't want to meet her glance. After a few quiet moments, the silence was broken.

"I'm sorry, Amanda, I suppose I should have told you that I was seeing Doctor Browne."

"No, no, it's no business of mine. We are still on good terms."

"I'm glad you think so. I mean, I know you are and I'm glad you're not angry."

"Of course not," Amanda answered, thinking to herself that Valerie was turning out to be a fast worker, as the expression went.

She picked up the telephone and called over to the Sons of Italy, hoping that De Luca was there so she could get details of the event and offer any assistance that might be needed.

"Miss Burnside. How nice of you to call. Everything is under control."

"Can we contribute anything? Refreshments, for example?"

"Not at all. As you can imagine, we are overflowing with donations from a grateful neighborhood. The bakery is sending cookies, we'd love to have wine, but naturally there will be a nonalcoholic punch. And you should see the lineup of entertainment. Music, singing, dancing. It will be quite a party."

It did sound like something new. Most ribbon cuttings she had heard of were dry affairs where the elected officials or donors stood around trying to look their best for the camera and dispersed shortly thereafter.

～

HALLORAN AND DOMINIC had a grimmer duty attending Giovanni Rinaldi's funeral. There had already been a visitation, then a rosary at the church the evening before, and now the event itself. It always struck Halloran as pointless to attend a funeral in the hopes of singling out a perpetrator, but it did give further insight into the relationships of the attendees.

The parents had settled on a High Mass, and the casket in front of the altar rail was surrounded by lilies, their cloying scent mixing with heavy incense in the crowded church. Despite someone having said that the family had fewer friends than most due to their province of origin, the pews were packed with older women dressed in black, their hair covered in veils or scarves. For these widows, a funeral was a social occasion and an opportunity to judge the wealth of their neighbors by the quality of the casket, the number of floral arrangements and the location of the grave site. Of course, everyone was buried in the same Catholic cemetery, but location was everything.

Halloran and Dominic sat in the last pew to observe the congregation.

"Wouldn't you know it's a High Mass. Just did one last Sunday" Dominic said.

"Your girlfriend has you go with her?"

"Yeah, she and her mother. The father stays at home and reads the newspapers. Says he has a beef with the Church about politics or something."

"Handy excuse. I'll have to try that one on my mother."

"With a brother who's a priest? Good luck with that."

Halloran shrugged. He no longer lived in his parents' home so the scrutiny of his comings and goings was a thing of the past. But his mother always managed to ask if he had attended Mass. To which he always responded, "Of course."

They watched the latecomers enter the church, crossing themselves as they made their way up the center aisle and squeezing into the end of a pew. A woman slipped into the space beside Halloran and kneeled, then crossed herself and sat back. He could not see her face as it was veiled, but he thought she was not young nor one of the widows and he caught the brief scent of some orange blossom cologne and shiny buckles on her shoes. No ring on her finger. Definitely not a widow.

The Mass dragged on, but before it was over, shunning protocol, the woman stood, genuflected, crossed herself and left abruptly. Halloran looked over at Dominic, who shrugged his shoulders. They both looked at her retreating figure and wondered who she might be.

They got up and began to follow her from a distance. She walked at a brisk pace and suddenly stopped and looked in a shop window. Halloran could have sworn that she gave them a sideways glance, though it was hard to tell because of the veil. She resumed walking but at a slower pace and when she got to the corner of the street, made a right and was out of sight for no more than a minute.

It was one minute too long. Halloran and Dominic stared down an empty street lined with shops and doorways that led up to second-story residences. They leapfrogged each other, looking into every other shop to be able to cover twice as many places than if they had gone together. She was in none of them.

They went into the last shop at the end of the street, a small grocery, and Dominic caught the eye of the man behind the counter.

"How do you get to the apartments upstairs?"

He pointed back to the way they had come.

They exited and, retracing their steps back to the other end of the street, saw a staircase up which opened onto the street but had no door. Ascending to the top of the stairs, they could see why. The apartments here all opened to a long hallway. Walking to the end they saw that there was an exit to the adjacent street.

"Okay, she pulled a fast one," Halloran said.

"She must live nearby if she knows about this setup. Maybe even lives in one of these," Dominic replied.

"She could. But not likely if she didn't want to have a conversation with us.

"Let's go back to the shop and see what's what," Halloran said. He hadn't planned on attending the interment anyway.

They walked through the blustery, crowded streets to the religious shop, which, of course, was closed. Taking the side street back to the alley, they surveyed the buildings that had visibility of the back of the shop. They knocked on the door of the first floor directly opposite repeatedly but got no answer. Moving one building down, they repeated the process, still with no results.

A woman opened a window above and shouted, "What do you want?"

"Does anybody live here, downstairs?"

She shrugged. "I hear people moving around, but I don't know who they are."

"May we come up and talk to you?"

She looked cautious, but seeing Dominic next to Halloran, she nodded her head, indicating it would be all right.

"The stairs are around to the right," she said, closing the window.

The stairs were wooden and damaged from the wet winter so that Halloran, the larger of the two detectives, wondered if he was going to plunge to the cement below. Yet the stairs held, and they got up to the second story where the woman held the door open for them.

The apartment was small, yet neat and warm, as they entered the kitchen. She offered them some coffee, which they refused, and motioned for them to sit at the bare, wooden kitchen table that likely had many functions for cooking, baking and eating.

"Thank you for letting us in," Halloran said, removing his hat and placing it on the table. Dominic kept his on.

"Did you know that the young man who worked in his father's shop across the alley was killed?" he asked.

"Who could have ignored it?" she said, patting her dark hair back into its bun at the back of her head, jiggling the gold earrings that pierced her ears. "The poor young man. The poor parents. How horrible!"

"You likely heard all the racket with screaming and the crowd and the police, but did you hear or see anything before that?"

"Ah, no. I have a young baby and he takes a midmorning nap, and sometimes I lie down next to him. It was the screaming that woke me up and I was afraid it was a fire or something. I looked out the window and saw all the people and the Rinaldis crying and wailing. Oh, what an awful thing to lose your child." Her eyes were wide with the imagining.

"Who lives downstairs?"

"I don't know. I don't think it's a family. I've only seen one man or another coming and going. The landlord would know."

Dominic pulled a small notepad from his pocket and a pencil from the other and asked, "What is the landlord's name?"

"I don't know. My husband made the lease. Somebody named Joey comes by once a week to collect the rent."

"Cash?" Halloran asked.

"Of course. Right after a Friday payday."

"Who lives next door to you?"

"On the second floor you mean?"

"Yes."

"No one. Well, sometimes I hear footsteps since our bedroom is next to that flat, but never anybody speaking. The wall is cold, so I don't think they even turn the heat on."

"That's strange."

"It is. It's like we're in this building all by ourselves. It's lonely without real neighbors. But we'll move out in a few months. That boy getting killed—that worries me and my husband, too."

"I can understand," Halloran said. He glanced around the small but immaculately clean kitchen with its Madonna on a shelf between the windows.

"Did that come from the store across the way?"

"Yes, isn't she beautiful? It came all the way from Italy."

"If you hear or see anything unusual, would you please contact us?" he asked, handing her a card with his name and phone number on it, although he doubted they had a phone.

They walked down the stairs and Halloran said, "I hate to do this, but I am dying to see the inside of the apartment next door. And I don't want to wait until the end of the week for some clown named Joey to let us in."

Dominic nodded and they went to the far end of the building and found another set of steps up to the second-floor apartment. They knocked on the door several times and then Halloran stood back, hiding Dominic, who was busy picking the lock, from view. They both looked around, making sure no one had seen them, and entered a kitchen much like the one next door except this had only a sink, a stove and an icebox. No table or chairs, but dirty curtains at the window blocking the view from the outside and cold as a tomb.

Dominic opened the icebox. It was empty of ice or food of any kind. Putting his hand over the stove, it was cool and all he felt was the cold air of the room since the heat wasn't on, just as the woman had said. Beyond the kitchen was a short hallway with a bathroom to the left and what must serve as a bedroom to the right although there was no furniture in it. At the end of the hall was a larger room, meant to be a living room or sitting room, again with no furniture, just dusty curtains and a vacant shallow fireplace meant for burning coal.

Halloran poked his shoe into the ashes of the fireplace. "Someone burned something in here. Odd, to not live in a place, to not furnish it, but to use it to burn some papers." He stooped down and poked at the ashes with a pencil he had taken from his breast pocket. "Not newspapers, but some kind of stapled pamphlet."

"This whole setup is strange," Dominic said. He stepped over to the window and moved a curtain aside with his index finger. "The only good thing about the place is that it's got a bird's eye view of the back of the shop."

Halloran joined him at the window to observe. "And what do you suppose young Giovanni or his father was up to that deserved surveillance? And by whom?"

## Chapter 10

Amanda had wanted to get flyers printed up announcing the opening of the clinic with the days and times that physicians would be available. One of De Luca's people, a young man named Bruno with a serious face and slicked-back hair, had written a translation of the information into Italian. He took both versions to a printer who had offered to provide the job at no cost and then make sure that the flyers were posted in as many shops and stores in the North End as possible. Additional flyers would be available at the ribbon cutting.

By the time the original got to the printer, it had been significantly edited and it was only when the printer called her to verify the spelling of some names that she realized what a public relations stunt this was going to be. The new wording indicated the Sons of Italy and the Mayor of Boston would be present to open the clinic for the neighborhood. No mention of Mr. Barlow or the Board of Directors of Mercy Hospital. That wouldn't do. She asked that he insert those words and then informed Miss Bailey that the Board needed to know about the Saturday event.

"Mr. Barlow, I hope that people don't think that the ribbon cutting means we're open for business that day."

"That would be awkward. No, we can't have all this hoopla and expect mothers to be bringing their sick children in at the same time. That would be a circus!" he laughed.

AMANDA AND MISS BAILEY got to the Sons of Italy building early that Saturday and the event looked like it might be just short of a circus. There were chairs lined up on the stage for the notable people, a podium, musicians seated in the front row of chairs, a group of girls in traditional clothing practicing twirling their skirts, several priests and a man who was laying out biscotti and cookies on trays. He turned to see the number of people coming in and looked stricken that he might not have brought enough. The chairs began to fill with families, shop owners —scores of people talking, laughing, calling out to each other.

Within a half hour, Salvatore de Luca came in with some kind of wide ribbon that hung from his right shoulder to his left hip fastened by a large pin as if he were royalty. Henry Rogers came in, scoped out the size of the crowd, exited, and minutes later came back following the Mayor, who shook hands with anybody who passed.

"Thank you for coming," he said to each one of them, although most wondered who he was and why he was welcoming them to their own neighborhood.

Amanda shook the Mayor's hand and then Henry's and went to the entrance, wondering what was keeping Mr. Barlow and the Board members. She saw that he was at the base of the steps standing next to the Board chair, Mrs. Tyrell, and that they appeared to be waiting for the others to arrive.

Where Amanda had at first been worried that not enough would attend, as the minutes passed and more of the Board members appeared, she began to wonder if there were enough chairs on the stage for them all. She caught the eye of Bruno, De Luca's assistant, who was surveying the number of people outside the building, and pointed to the group that was assembling. He nodded and went back inside to attend to it.

To her relief, Fred, the resident and a nurse, all in uniform, also appeared and she thought how wise it was to present them to the assembly. If only the resident could be Italian, but they couldn't make an adjustment at this point. The fact that they had come and looked so professional added greatly to the event.

Fred's eyebrows rose as he saw how many people were there.

"I'm afraid we're going to be overwhelmed come Tuesday," he said.

"I don't think everyone here is a potential patient. After all, the clinic is just for families with children."

"But look at all the families," the nurse said.

"And look at all the children," Wilkinson added.

It was the first time Amanda began to realize the enormity of the situation and wondered if there was some way to halt the tidal wave of people that might show up the following week. Ask them to call for appointments? No, that was ridiculous. Many people didn't have telephones and who were they supposed to call? That would entail one person's time on their end to juggle all that. And what about the language issue? That took her mind in another direction: should she have thought of having a translator available? She would ask Bruno about that and for propriety's sake, the person would have to be a woman.

"Well, well, look what you've done here," Mrs. Tyrell said to Amanda as she walked into the building and saw the crowd.

"It's hardly all my doing, I can assure you," she responded. "Mr. De Luca is the one who spearheaded this gathering."

"Impressive," she heard another Board member say as he smiled and nodded to those who were already seated, waiting for the show to begin.

De Luca was now at the podium; luckily someone had provided a microphone because he never would have been heard over the din of the crowd. He tapped on it, which made loud thumping noises that quelled the talking momentarily.

"*Buon giorno!*" he said with his arms outstretched as if to embrace the entirety of the room.

Henry had seated the Mayor dead center of the chairs on the stage and Mr. Barlow was leading the Board members to fill the remaining seats. De Luca was nodding and waving to people in the crowd and motioning them to be seated. Gradually the noise subsided, and it was very quiet except for some young children and babies who could not be silenced.

"We are here today to dedicate the opening of a new clinic for the children of our neighborhood." Clapping.

"I, Salvatore De Luca, heard of the need for medical services for our young children and the long journey to Mercy Hospital. We must be grateful for the effort of our Mayor and the Board of the hospital for making this happen." He turned and applauded the others on the stage and the audience did the same.

"But first, before we begin, let's appreciate the glorious voice of Signora Orsini, who has performed at La Scala and many other notable locations in Italy, Europe and the United States. She will lead us in the national anthem."

It was at this point that Amanda realized she had only planned up to the event happening, not how it would play out. She had no idea that there would be an opera singer, but there she was, just as one would picture a soprano: statuesque with a large bosom, wearing a long dress with her hair in braids wrapped around her head. She stepped up to the microphone and looked to the musicians for her cue.

The crowd stood up. The introductory notes were played, and she filled the space with her powerful voice.

Miss Bailey's eyes almost popped out of her head. "Gosh, is that what opera is like?" she said, never having attended.

"Yes," said Amanda, who had, but had never experienced the amplification that made a voice ricochet around the room. When the Signora finished and bowed, the crowd applauded for several minutes and she had to take another curtain call, although no curtain was employed.

De Luca stepped up to the microphone again and cleared his throat. "Good friends and neighbors, esteemed guests, welcome to the Sons of Italy Hall." Some from the audience applauded. "Before we begin, Father Palladino from St. Lorenzo's Church is here to give a blessing to our endeavor." Everyone stood again.

"In the name of the Father, the Son and the Holy Ghost." That was the shortest sentence he uttered as he then launched into a flowery speech about God, the sacred trust of the family, keeping one's spiritual and physical health for the sake of God and the community.

Miss Bailey was shifting from foot to foot and, like Amanda, was probably wondering where this speech was going. The only place it went was on and on, invoking God many times to bless the building, the organization, the United States, Massachusetts, Boston, the neighborhood, the families, the businesses and all the supporters of the venture at hand. Then he remembered that doctors and nurses and the hospital were to be blessed as well as everyone else who worked there, the miracles of modern medicine and the people who developed them. At this point, he stopped, not for effect but because either he lost his train of thought or had run out of people and entities to bless.

"Amen," someone from the crowd said, a sentiment echoed throughout the auditorium and with shuffling of feet, everyone sat down.

The priest made the sign of the cross in front of the group and sat down.

"Phew," Miss Bailey said. "I thought he was going to go one more round."

"Thank you, Father Palladino. And we are blessed today with so many prominent people here to share in our good fortune. First, Mr. Barlow of Mercy Hospital." He stood, smiled and sat down. Reading from note cards, De Luca called out each of the Board members by name and they in turn stood and smiled or nodded to the crowd, which dutifully applauded. "And now, a few words from our Mayor." More applause.

The Mayor stood up slowly, nodding his head in response to the clapping. He had a folksy way about him, leaning one arm across the podium and speaking without notes. After thanking them for coming out in such great numbers to see him, he began to tell his Horatio Alger story of starting out in life as the youngest son of a poor Irish family. Clearly, he was trying to impart to his audience the notion that anyone in America could make it to the top if they had the gumption and work ethic that he had developed early in life.

From time to time during his long tirade, women got up and took children downstairs to use the restrooms, restless people rustled in their seats and one poor man tried to stifle a sneezing attack, which drew some soft chuckles from the crowd. In addition, latecomers crept in and wandered around, looking for a vacant seat.

But the Mayor kept talking, ignoring the restless dance troupe that waited at the sidelines towards the back, a few of them twirling their skirts in boredom.

"And so, friends…," the Mayor was at last coming to the summing up of his lengthy remarks that had begun at his ignoble birth and were about to lead up to his rise to the top when the sound of metal rattling came from the back of the room where something had been hurled through the front doors.

Everyone looked around and then the object started smoking and, as one, the crowd lurched forward, seeking to escape what everyone thought must be a bomb. There was nowhere for everyone to go except onto the stage, some leaping up, others holding a hand out to help others. Mothers were screaming, holding their children to their breasts, men were shouting and dashing to the sides of the stage where there were steps that led to a back area, and the esteemed guests who had been seated either got up or were pushed out of the way by the frightened mass of people.

The can continued to emit smoke and then abruptly stopped and someone laughed. "It's a smoke bomb!"

More yelling and screaming ensued at the word 'bomb' but Henry, who had been in the wings all that time, pushed his way forward and said, "It's a smoke bomb. It's harmless. Some kid probably threw it in to cause mischief."

The Mayor hadn't moved from the podium during the entire event, but then De Luca stepped up and nudged him out of the way. "I'd say it's time for our folk dancers!" he said in a cheery voice.

The children, who had been at the back of the room and most immediately disturbed by the incident, were stock-still and only brought to life by the authoritative short claps of their instructor, a woman with a fierce set of eyebrows.

"Come now, take your places. Maestro?" she cued the musicians, who began to play. The children were slow to get into the rhythm of the music but as an accordion began to play, they cheered up and got into the swing of things. Some of the audience began to clap in time to the music and the skirts spun and smiles returned to their faces.

When the dance was over, the audience applauded, laughed and called out in appreciation and relief that it was only a smoke bomb and not a real one, and the dancers stopped and headed for the refreshments.

Amanda hadn't realized that Miss Bailey had her arm in a death grip from the time the can had rolled into the room until the dance ended and people clapped. Henry had flown past them and out the front doors during the dance performance and he was just coming in as the multitude surrounded the tables where the food had been laid out.

"Henry, what did you see?"

"It wasn't some young kid who did this. They were grown men. And I'd like to know who tried to start what could have been a riot."

# Chapter 11

Amanda battled the relieved throng descending from the stage and the steps to either side of it, Miss Bailey in her wake, to make sure that the Board members had not been squashed, trampled or traumatized by the recent scare. Mrs. Tyrell had a stiff smile on her face, but her eyes were still wide, and she took Amanda's hands in her own.

"Are things always like this here?" she asked in a low voice, the smile in place lest anyone overhear her.

"I couldn't say. It's a lively neighborhood, but I've never experienced a smoke bomb before."

The several male Board members were not making any pretense of being unfazed; some were scowling, and others muttered among themselves. Amanda hoped this didn't spell the dissolution of the clinic before it had even begun.

From backstage she could hear the Mayor and De Luca in a loud argument; she ushered the Board members off the stage to prevent them hearing more—and so she could listen in.

"How dare you attempt to humiliate me in such a public way?" the Mayor said. "A smoke bomb! Is that your people's idea of a joke? It scared the wits out of many people. Children could have been trampled in the melee."

"This was not my doing, of course. There are forces in the neighborhood who don't want outside help. They may be frightened of the influence of other cultures."

"What the hell does that mean?"

"Some people want to keep their own customs, their own foods, the old ways."

"So, they don't really want to be Americans, is that it?"

"No, no. They want to be both. Keep their regional dishes, their dialects, their sense of Italian independence and still be Americans."

"Well, they can't be both. You and I know what is going on in Italy right now. Independence? It's a dictatorship. More oppressive than having a royal family."

"Not everyone is happy with what is happening in Italy right now. Some people are. That's the problem."

"You need to get to the bottom of this. You've got your ear to the ground. Find out who did this. And be in my office Monday morning. I'll have the police force investigate this. And where the hell are the police?" he shouted.

The Mayor came out from behind the rear curtain and momentarily looked embarrassed to know that his conversation may have been overheard by Amanda, but put a brave face on it and repeated, "Where are the police?" to Henry who had come up onto the stage.

"Someone must have called them. They'll be here in a few minutes, I think."

"Don't let anybody near that thing! It might explode!" the Mayor insisted as he saw a group of young boys poking at the can with their feet. Two mothers came up, batting the boys on the side of the head and dragging them away.

Henry rushed down to the object and stood by it, protecting it until the police could show up. That turned out to be Dominic, who came quickly into the building, his overcoat flapping about his legs.

"What's going on here?" he asked Henry, who provided him with the necessary details.

Dominic poked at the can with his foot before putting his gloved hand down on it to see if it was hot or about to ignite again.

"It's a smoke bomb," he said.

"I know what that is," Henry said peevishly. "We want to know where it came from—who tossed it in here and why."

They glared at each other.

"Do you imagine there are fingerprints on it or something? Were there people outside? Did they see anything?"

"How should I know? You're the detective, aren't you? What's your name by the way?"

Dominic opened his overcoat to show his badge. "My name is Dominic Barone. I'm a detective with the Boston police." His chin jutted out as he spoke.

"I think the Mayor is going to want to talk to you people after you do a thorough investigation."

"What if it was some kids trying to be funny?" Dominic said.

"A packed room with families and children? What's funny about that? People were scared. Look, that doctor is even treating somebody over there who may have had a heart attack."

Their attention was taken by Fred and the resident kneeling beside a seated woman who fanned her face with one of the flyers and looked distressed. Someone had provided the woman with a glass of water, and she seemed to gradually gain her composure.

"We'll want to see you and the Chief very soon, I can assure you," Henry said, poking his index finger in the other man's chest. Henry walked away to look for the Mayor.

Amanda approached Dominic. "I guess you're on duty today," she said.

"Lucky me," he responded. "I take it you were here during all this business."

"I'm afraid so. I don't know if it was a prank, but it scared the heck out of all these people. Me included."

Miss Bailey came up at that moment and there was an electric moment when she and Dominic exchanged glances. Amanda introduced them and, feeling awkward, left to speak to Fred, whose patient seemed to have been revived.

"Fred, I'm so sorry. What a scene!"

"Is it always like this?"

"What do you mean? You've been to the North End many times, not just for a wonderful meal, haven't you?"

"Yes, but not to a large gathering where people panic and where there could have been crowd-induced injuries."

She looked around at the crowd gathered at the tables, chatting, drinking coffee and eating pastries. "It seems to have calmed down already. I'm sorry they didn't get to introduce you and your staff, however."

Fred's jaw tightened. "Be that as it may. We'll be here on Tuesday, and I hope nothing of the sort will take place at that time. If I or my staff are endangered in any way, that's the end of the clinic."

The crowd had thinned, and most had left after an eventful afternoon. Amanda wandered over to the refreshments table with the hopes of getting at least one cookie but found that everything had been eaten with only crumbs left behind. The baker shrugged his shoulders in mute apology and asked if she would like some coffee. But when he tipped the urn, only a few drops came out.

"We had a lot of people here," he said apologetically.

"Thank you, anyway." All she could think of was finding Miss Bailey so they could both go home, and she could put her feet up and read.

Miss Bailey was still in conversation with Dominic and, while Amanda would rather not interrupt, her feet hurt, she was thirsty and dog-tired, so she wanted to collect her friend and head out. There was an awkward moment as she approached and said, "I think we can go now."

Miss Bailey looked at Dominic and he at her and jumped to the rescue.

"I'd be happy to give you a ride home," he said.

Amid the stammers and blushes and inquiring looks, it was agreed that the couple would leave together, and Amanda was free for the afternoon.

When she arrived home, her first thought was because the house was quiet, her parents must be out and she could retreat to her room and possibly take a nap. But no sooner had she taken some steps than her mother appeared in the sitting room below.

"Amanda! We've got a letter from Louisa already." She waved the thin blue airmail paper in her hand. "Come read what she's been doing."

But rather than allowing her to read, her mother gave her the details while glancing at the writing. "She's been out to Fort Sumter by boat! And they're touring some plantation this coming week." She turned the page and skimmed it. "The house they're staying in is on the Battery, whatever that is, and she said it's beautiful and the family has many servants."

"That should make things comfortable for her. Does she mention any beaches or sunbathing?"

"No, but I'm sure they'll do that. I'm so glad she is having a wonderful time. And no mention of you-know-who."

"Of course not, Mother. He's the last person she would refer to in a letter home." Amanda wondered what the airmail letter to Rob was like. Probably not full of the excitement of being somewhere new and enchanting but likely how dull everything was and wishing she were in Boston.

"I'll read it later, thank you." She climbed the stairs, took off her shoes and lay down on the bed with the latest mystery book, "The Thirteen Problems," a collection of stories that she hoped would put her to sleep after she finished the first one.

It was not to be.

She heard her mother come up the stairs and then approach her door, knock and come in, her face contorted in distress.

"Whatever is the matter?" Amanda asked.

"Nora is gone."

"Gone? What happened to her?"

Her mother sat on the bed. "She's leaving on rather short notice, I must say. She just told me that she has been offered a job at City Hall, of all things."

"As a secretary?"

"Yes, how do you know?"

"I saw her practicing typewriting. I suppose it was inevitable."

"Oh, what are we going to do? Mary already has a sour face imagining that all the work will fall to her."

"Just for a short time, until you find a replacement. When does Nora leave?"

"Tomorrow is her last day. Her last half day, that is. It is most inconsiderate of her."

"That is short notice," Amanda said. "I hope you'll still give her a good recommendation if it is asked for. She has done excellent work."

"Then why is she leaving?"

Amanda patted her mother on the arm. "She's young and she doesn't want to be a maid forever, that's why. I'm sure the new job pays better and there may be chance for advancement."

"Oh, you young girls and your ideas of working and a career. I do disapprove," her mother said, getting up.

"You'll find somebody, I'm sure."

"Whom I'll have to train…." Her shoulders slumped in anticipation of breaking in somebody new. She ended with her familiar lament, "It's always something, isn't it?"

HALLORAN WAS NOT HAVING a good Saturday afternoon, either. He had gone into work with the idea of finishing up some paperwork that he could leave on the secretary's desk to type up. Although there were plenty of officers working on Saturdays, they were mostly deployed in anticipation of the usual round of brawls, family altercations and random violence that peppered the weekends. But the office staff only worked Monday through Friday, so he was spared the chatter, the drop-ins from other offices and the noise of the typewriters and telephones ringing. If they rang at all, the operator fielded them downstairs.

He had barely got his thoughts together on a burglary case when he sensed someone coming down the hall and put his head up to see the unhappy face of the Police Chief.

Halloran screwed the cap back on his pen and gave the man his full attention.

"What do you think of this Dominic Barone?"

That wasn't what Halloran had anticipated to be the opening line. "I think he is capable and hard-working. And he knows the North End. Why, what's the matter?"

"The Mayor's the matter." The Chief remained standing, which was never a good sign.

"The Mayor went to some event in the Sons of Italy Hall and a smoke bomb was thrown into the room."

Halloran's eyes widened. "A bomb? Or a smoke bomb? Is everyone okay?"

"Nobody injured. But the Mayor's ego has been badly damaged. Evidently, he was just getting into the swing of things with his speech when it went off and that was the end of him being able to talk. There was pandemonium and when things calmed down, everybody left."

"Who told you this?"

"That sawed-off, know-it-all Henry what's-his-name who works for him was on the horn as soon as the dust cleared. And he wants Dominic on the carpet tomorrow morning."

"It's Sunday. It's his day off. Why Dominic?"

"I know it's Sunday. But he's to be at the Mayor's office at 10 a.m. sharp. And he better not consider it to be working overtime. And why? Because he was on duty today."

"I know that," Halloran said.

"The Mayor, or at least his little shadow, thinks that he should have either prevented it from happening or have caught the perpetrators by now."

"That's asking a lot." Seeing the Chief's scowl, he amended his comment. "If you don't mind me saying so."

The Chief pointed his index finger at Halloran. "I do mind you saying so. Because it's not your place to do so. And as his more experienced partner, you'll be there, too."

In response to the pained look on Halloran's face, he continued. "And don't give me any malarkey about having to go to Mass with your ailing mother. I know she is in perfect health, and you haven't been going to Mass much lately anyway." He stalked out of the room, leaving Halloran to wonder how the Chief knew such things. Sometimes Boston was a small town, indeed.

## Chapter 12

Halloran called Dominic at home that afternoon to inform him of the meeting with the Mayor the next day. His partner was silent for a few moments.

"Do you think he's going to fire me?"

"Probably not. He just wants to chew somebody out and we'll be there to take it from him."

"But there was nothing more I could have done. I was blocks away dealing with some kid who had snatched a piece of fruit from Conte's stall outside his shop. Somebody came running down the street yelling about a bomb, so I left the kid and the grocer and ran to the Hall. There was nobody outside, just a lot of noise and residual smoke coming from the building, but nobody lurking around to see the effect of their actions, I can tell you. By the time I figured out it was harmless and went outside again to check, there was still nobody there except anxious neighbors who heard the commotion."

Halloran sighed. "I don't doubt you, but the Mayor has to chew somebody out and we'll just sit there and take it. It will blow over. Just don't argue with the man—that will only prolong the agony."

"Okay."

"Sorry, buddy. We'll get through this."

Dominic hung up and Halloran decided to go home. On second thought, he decided to go up to the North End and ask around. The man who sold newspapers on the corner of Hanover Street had sold most of his evening newspapers and was starting to close up, but Halloran came up and bought the last one.

"Heard about all that racket at the Sons of Italy this afternoon?" he asked as he handed him the money.

"Couldn't hear it from here, but a bunch of folks told me about it later. Stupid punks."

"You think it was kids who did it?"

"Who knows? That Sal fellow rubs a lot of people the wrong way."

"You think somebody did it to embarrass him?"

He shrugged.

A woman came up, standing a few feet away and perused the newspapers. As Halloran looked down at his, he noticed the buckles on her shoes. He began to walk past her and caught the scent of orange blossom cologne.

The woman at the funeral.

He waited until she paid for her paper before stopping her.

"I think I need to talk to you."

She looked alarmed and glanced at the vendor as if asking for his help.

He shook his head with a wry smile. "Forget about it. He's a cop."

Rather than reassuring her with his words, she dropped the paper and began to run down the street but tripped and landed on her knees with a cry.

"You made me ruin my stockings!" she shouted.

He helped her to her feet. "I'm not arresting you unless you think there is some reason I ought to."

She glared at him and examined the holes in the knees of her stockings and her scuffed shoes.

"Why did you give me the flit?"

"I don't like strange men following me."

"How did you know Giovanni?"

"Who?"

"Come on. Giovanni. Some folks called him Johnny."

"Oh, him. He was a friend of my brother's."

"Who's your brother."

"Why do you want to know?"

"We can do this back at the station if you like."

"No." She looked around and saw the vendor watching and listening.

"Come with me." She led him across the wide street where the traffic had calmed down because of approaching dinner time. The shops and stores were closing for the night, too, with the metal awnings being pulled down to protect the windows and the merchandise inside until Monday.

It was clear she did not want to lead him on a direct path to her destination, perhaps hoping to confuse him or baffle the vendor, who now looked around the corner of his shed to follow the action. They went up Hanover, down a side street, into the alley, back into another side street farther away and then backtracked to the long alley where the Rinaldis lived at the other end.

She took him up to the second floor, walking quietly and holding her finger to her lips that he should not talk. "Busybodies," she whispered. She opened the door to a small apartment and turned on the light, revealing a sparsely furnished room and one of the few he had seen without a religious picture on the wall.

Without sitting, she said, "What do you want?"

"What's your name?"

She paused.

"Your real name. I can ask around…."

"Maria Ricci."

"Is your brother Mario at home?"

"What? Oh, no, he's away right now."

"Okay, Mrs. Ricci, there is no brother, is there?"

She stared at him. "No. So, I know you're a cop and now you know I'm a liar. How about a drink?"

It wasn't the response he was expecting but he said, "Sure, why not. What do you have?"

If she thought she was going to soften him up or something, she had another thing coming.

"It's rye. It's not too bad. I work at a club, and it was my Christmas bonus." She walked over to a far corner of the room and pulled back a curtain that hid the kitchenette, took out two glasses and a bottle from the cabinet and came back to the living room. "Have a seat." He sat and took off his hat. She poured two fingers-worth and touched his glass with hers.

"Salute," he said.

"I'm not Italian. That was my husband's name."

"Is your husband at home?"

"He left a couple of years ago. Took off on one of the boats. Haven't seen him since."

She took a gulp of the alcohol.

"Okay, so tell me about Giovanni."

She looked down at her glass and bit her lip. "We used to talk." She looked at him directly. "Are you a prude?"

"I don't think so."

"Okay, so then he started coming around. You know. Typical Old Country family, their noses in his business all the time. He was unhappy working for his father. A demanding man, from what he said. Always complaining about his workmanship."

Halloran remembered his father praising his work. Probably didn't want to tell him to his face lest he get a swelled head.

"Then he dragged him into all that political business."

Halloran waited for her to explain, but she let it hang.

"A turf war with the gangs?"

"No, you know, who should run Italy."

Halloran thought back to the father who made it seem like Italian politics were of no interest to him at all. Maybe the son took a different turn.

"Did he mention anyone who wanted to harm him?"

"Just that boy his sister was seeing. Sneaking behind her parents' back. He decided to have some words with the guy, and it became more than that. Threw a couple of punches at each other. Nothing too serious. I patched him up and he thought up some story to tell his father about it."

"Were you seeing him up until the time he died?"

"We had cooled it a bit. One of the nosy neighbors saw him coming up here once and threatened to make a big deal of it."

"How?"

"Blab to her friends. Said she'd tell the father, too. He would go out with some girl from time to time. But he always came back to me." She downed the remainder of her drink. "Aren't you going to have any?" she asked, looking at his untouched glass.

"No, but thanks for the hospitality. And the information." He got up and put his hat back on. "If you think of anything else, please call me." He handed her his card and left.

She glanced at the card and tossed it on the table. Then she sat back on the sofa, took his glass and sipped from it while she wondered what she should do.

## Chapter 13

Halloran was dreading Sunday morning. Didn't the Mayor have something better to do than drag two detectives into his palatial office—and having seen it once before, he could attest that it was impressive—to chew them out about something that they couldn't possibly have prevented? Then the thought hit him that if the Mayor was taking communion that morning, he would not have had anything to eat. Great. So hungry and cranky on top of everything else.

He made himself a cup of coffee, something he had still not mastered since moving out to live on his own. It was either too strong or too weak, but at least it was hot. He made himself some toast and looked in the icebox for butter. None. He ate the dry bread by dunking it in the coffee. Not good. He was just going to have to learn how to fend for himself. It had taken long enough to move out of his parents' home into one side of the duplex the family owned, and he was not going to give up his freedom for the sake of a decent breakfast. Even if the amenities at his family's home were better, the incessant noise of people talking or arguing, the racket of his sister's baby, the constant stream of neighbors or friends had persuaded him that moving out was worth it. Even if it meant paying rent, which by duty he felt he needed to do. When he had lived at home, his working hours had always put his mother in a tizzy, wondering if something bad had happened because he didn't come and go at regular hours.

This day was certainly not regular hours, and he was annoyed at the entire scenario. He brushed down his suit, put on his overcoat and hat and drove to City Hall. Being a Sunday, he could park right out front and, trotting to the front doors, found they were locked. Could this be a last-minute redemption? He peered in the glass and saw that there was someone on duty inside who waddled to the doors and asked him his name before letting him in. Dominic was already there, looking sick.

"He said to wait here until he came back down," the guard said without elaborating on who the 'he' was."

There were benches in the lobby and they sat down. Dominic looked shell-shocked, and Halloran said, "It'll be over before you know it."

They waited about twenty minutes. Finally, the elevator pinged and the Police Chief came out. He scowled at the two detectives, who jumped to their feet. He stood looking them up and down.

"Well, my fine fellows. I have just saved you from the ire of the Mayor. I talked him down and let him know that you two were going to get to the bottom of this. He did not relish being made a fool of in the North End. So, you will do your best to find the felons or somebody who fits the description of who might do such a thing and bring them to justice. Understood?"

"Yes, Sir," they said in unison.

"And get the hell out of here before he changes his mind and comes down here."

"Yes, Sir," they said again. They moved swiftly to the doors and went quickly down the front steps.

"Come on, let's have a decent breakfast to celebrate," Halloran said, clapping Dominic on the back. "I know a wonderful, greasy diner."

"Gosh, that was awfully nice of the Chief to intercede for us."

Halloran stopped to look the younger man in the eye. "I don't think the Mayor was as upset as the Chief made out. He just wants to hold something against us for future reference. Just wait and see."

AMANDA WOKE TO ANOTHER COLD, blustery day and couldn't help feeling deep envy for her sister, lounging in the sunshine. She said as much to her father as he read the paper at the breakfast table.

"Cheer up, it looks like their temperatures are only in the fifties today in Charleston."

"Really? I thought it would be warmer. Still, those are spring temperatures for us."

"Amanda, if you really wanted to go South for a bit, we could manage it."

"Thanks, Daddy. But I'm too involved in work to do that. And can you imagine swanning into the clinic in the North End in the middle of winter and telling everyone that I was going on a vacation?"

Mrs. Burnside emerged from the kitchen and looked at her watch. "Hurry up, you two, or we'll be late for church. Cook is in a real mood today," she added in a whisper.

"Still upset about Nora leaving?"

"Yes and making no bones about it to the girl. The least she could do is be gracious to her on her last day here." She looked at her husband. "Do you have the envelope?"

Without looking up, he patted his breast pocket. "We'll give it to her before we go out. She'll be gone by the time we get back."

Amanda wasn't sure she should mention it but forged ahead anyway. "I know of a young woman who might be interested in working here."

"Really? Oh, dear. She isn't some poor person who can't find work elsewhere, is she?"

"The girl I'm thinking of is working for her parents at the moment, but she might be interested in a paying position."

"Where does she work now?"

"Her parents run an Italian restaurant."

"Oh, dear. That won't work. I'm sure Cook will feel threatened."

"She's not the cook at the restaurant; her mother is the chef. She's been helping take orders and serving the patrons."

Mrs. Burnside paused. "Do you think she would be suitable?"

"Of course! Does she want to be a maid? That I don't know. But I can certainly ask her. She just graduated from high school and would probably like to be out on her own."

"Well then, all right."

They finished their meal and Nora came into the breakfast room to clear the plates.

"Just a moment," Mr. Burnside said.

She stopped what she was doing.

"We just wanted to say that we have appreciated your work here and wish you all the luck in your new position. Here's a token of our appreciation." He handed her the envelope and she looked surprised and then her eyes welled up.

"Thank you both."

"Just remember to put in a good word for us at City Hall," he added.

She laughed, wiped her eyes and thanked them again.

"So many changes," Mrs. Burnside muttered.

"Mother, if it would ease your mind, I could go talk to her today and see if she is interested. If not, you could contact an agency tomorrow."

Her mother looked at her husband and hesitated. "Just suggest it to her, won't you? I wouldn't like to make her an offer before meeting her to see if she'd be suitable."

"Of course. I'll go now."

"And miss church?"

"You know which is more important," Amanda said.

The truth was she wasn't looking forward to bumping into Fred or anyone else who might know that they weren't seeing one another. And what if he were there escorting Valerie? Everybody would assume Amanda had been jilted. It was best she occupy herself with something to do instead of sitting in a pew wondering if people were looking at her.

The streets were almost empty of cars in Beacon Hill and looked even emptier in the North End since most of the shops were closed. She wondered if she had miscalculated and Catalano's restaurant might be shut as well seeing the closed sign behind the glass on the front door. Putting her hands to each side of her eyes, she looked into the dark room and saw that Mr. Catalano and Simona were putting tablecloths out and setting the tables for an after-church lunch crowd. She tapped on the glass, and they looked up in surprise.

Simona opened the door and let her in.

"We're not officially open until noon. Blue Laws, you know," she said.

"Of course. I wanted to talk to you if you are free for a few minutes."

They sat down at a table. "I overheard your father talking to the two detectives the other day about how you were looking for a job. We have a position for a maid open at our house and I was wondering if you might be interested."

Simona looked up in surprise. "A housemaid?"

"Yes." Then Amanda thought perhaps the girl would be offended by the suggestion.

"I don't know what a housemaid does, exactly. We don't have one. We do everything ourselves," she said with a laugh.

"It's about tidying up, answering the door, light dusting—someone comes in twice a week for the heavy cleaning—making beds, serving meals, that sort of thing. Helping Cook although she does all the meal preparation."

Simona thought it over.

"What if you met with my mother tomorrow and she could explain what the job entails, the hours and how much it pays?"

"All right. Thank you for asking. I would be happy to meet with her."

"Here's the address," Amanda said, scribbling it on a piece of paper she pulled out of her handbag. "I'd better be going. Busy week with the clinic opening on Tuesday."

"I hope you don't take this the wrong way," Simona said. "But people here are very religious, and it might be a good idea to have a Madonna in the clinic."

"Oh, I hadn't even thought of that." Amanda looked around for guidance on what to do next.

"I'm sure Mr. Rinaldi would be happy to sell you one. His shop is open today after Mass. It's when people tend to buy such things."

"Good idea," Amanda said and thanked her.

She left feeling awkward about offering the job interview in the first place, not knowing if the girl was insulted, genuinely interested or just trying to appease her. Now, she was going to a shop that sold Catholic religious items and hadn't the slightest idea of how to phrase what she was looking for. Should she ask for a saint and hope for the best or a Madonna, which was like the big guns, if she understood their faith correctly.

On the one hand, she wanted to do everything correctly, but on the other she was hoping that Rinaldi's shop was closed; but as she walked in that direction, she could see people entering. She gulped and kept her head up and thought of how best to phrase it.

The bell tinkled as she entered the shop and the owner looked up from wrapping something at the counter.

"Good day, Miss," he said, and the customer turned to see who had come in. "I'll be with you in a moment."

Only having been to a Catholic Mass once, Amanda was not sure what she would find in the store, but it was evidently meant for lay people, not priests, as there were no vestments, robes or communion cups. She wandered around the aisles looking at small bottles and realized they were intended for holy water. Next to them were semicircular cups labeled as fonts, some with images of saints or a crucifix as a backdrop. There was an entire shelf display of candles, some with decals of saints, Jesus or Mary, others with bands around them labeled 'Lenten Candles,' as well as sets of Advent candles, although she knew it was certainly not that time of year. Perhaps best to stock up early.

The bell pinged and she felt the owner come up alongside her. He smiled and then recognizing her, his face collapsed. "You were here…."

"I'm sorry, I didn't mean to distress you. And I'm so sorry about your son."

He nodded.

"I'm with the hospital group that is sponsoring the clinic at the Sons of Italy Hall, and it was suggested to me that we have some type of religious statue present." She looked at him for a reaction to make sure she wasn't mistaken.

"Oh yes, of course. So many to choose from. You know, of course, that Saint Nicholas is the patron saint of children." He picked up a statue and held it with both hands.

She laughed. "Of course, Saint Nick."

His face was serious. "He was a devout person who gave gifts to children and money to young women for dowries. Now he is Santa Claus!" He put Saint Nicholas back and led her to another display. "Saint Joseph is also popular when he is depicted as holding Our Lord as a baby."

"That's very nice. And I heard your son created these?"

"Yes. An excellent craftsman," he said.

Amanda continued up and down the aisles and then her eyes landed on a large Madonna, about a foot high, that was behind the counter. "Oh, I think I'd like that one," she said, moving closer.

"So sorry, that one is not for sale," he said.

"Whyever not? I saw so many of them in the workshop that were broken. Surely you have more?"

"I'm sorry, that one is not for sale. It is the only one that survived the attack on my son. And we're waiting for the next shipment," he added.

"Of course, I understand."

The bell pinged again, and he smiled at the woman who entered with two children.

"I'll continue to look around," Amanda said, allowing him to attend to a familiar customer.

She got to the end of one aisle and looked up at the crucifix display on the wall. Something was off. The wall was not exactly straight level and it made the display look odd. She backed away to the end of the aisle as if to contemplate the items and noticed that from the entry to the back workshop there was a blocked-off space of several feet as if there were a closet in between. Perhaps a restroom?

Amanda sensed that the owner was observing her, and she picked up a devotional book of some sort, turning the pages but looking at the floor adjacent to the crucifix wall. There was a small gap at the end where the owner's space behind the counter met the wall. Was something behind there? She looked up and he looked away quickly. She picked up the largest Saint Joseph and approached him.

"I think this will be perfect."

"I agree. Excuse me," he said to the other customer and took the saint behind the counter and began to wrap him in paper. "You should have him blessed by the priest for extra measure," he said.

"This must be an old building. Have you been here long?"

"I came to this country a long time ago and worked for the man who had this store. When he got older, he sold the business to me. Nothing has changed since then."

"No need for unnecessary changes," she agreed. He rang up the sale and escorted her to the front door, almost anxious to have her leave.

"Thank you for your advice," she said.

When she got home, her mother, noticing the package, asked if she had been shopping.

"Just a little homecoming present for the new clinic location," Amanda said.

The telephone rang and the operator asked if she would accept a collect call from Charleston.

"Oh, yes," Amanda said, motioning her mother over to the chair next to the telephone table. "Hello, Louisa. How are you?"

"You don't need to shout," her sister said. "That's what the telephone is for."

"You're calling a bit early, aren't you?"

"We're going out to a concert in a few hours. I don't know how late that will go, so I wanted to call now."

Mrs. Burnside was waving her hand at Amanda, wanting to get a chance to speak.

"Here's Mother," Amanda said, allowing her mother to sit down while she bent over to put her ear on the other side of the receiver to listen in.

"Hello, darling. How is everything?"

"Just marvelous. You can't imagine how lovely this city is, so charming and what a social life these people lead! There is something to do every day, whether a little concert in someone's home or a tea dance. We even took a little boat trip up the Ashley River to tour one of the oldest plantations in the area." They could hear her ask a question to someone before resuming her narrative. "It's called Middleton and it gorgeous. Beautiful gardens—although not much was in bloom, as you can imagine—and an extraordinary house. Although it seems much of the main building suffered damage during the Civil War."

"Don't forget what side we were on, Louisa," her sister reminded her.

"Do you know that some people have asked if I am related to a General Burnside?" Louisa lowered her voice to a whisper. "Are we?"

"I believe a distant relation. Pay them no heed. The war has long been over. What sort of concert can there be on a Sunday evening?" Mrs. Burnside asked.

"It's in an old church down by the market. Some cadets from the Citadel will be escortin' us."

"Are you getting a Southern accent already?" Amanda accused her.

"Don't be silly. Anyway, this call is probably costing a fortune. Give Daddy a kiss and I'll write again soon."

Mrs. Burnside ended the call with admonitions about proper behavior and making sure she thanked the hostess for her kindness. She sat for a moment with a small wrinkle between her eyes.

"Sounds like she's having a grand time. What is it?"

"I just hope she doesn't come home engaged to someone."

Amanda laughed. "Wouldn't that be better than her current romantic interest here?"

"I don't want to think about it," her mother said, bustling off to the sitting room.

Amanda thought that it was funny that her mother didn't want to think of her daughters getting married, yet at the same time worried that they were still single.

When her mother was well out of earshot, she dialed Halloran's office number. It rang several times, and she realized it was Sunday and he would likely not be in the office. To her surprise, he answered.

"Oh," was her opening remark.

"Oh—who is this?" he asked sternly.

"It's Amanda. Hello, I didn't know if you would be in." She suddenly thought herself forward and ridiculous to have called him and was silent.

"I have the feeling you have something to tell me."

"Yes, I do, but maybe this is not important, or I was imagining it," she said, feeling herself blushing.

"Well?"

"I was in Rinaldi's shop a little while ago, buying a saint."

"Are you thinking of converting?" he asked.

"Don't be funny. I was buying it for the clinic. I was persuaded to purchase something to give the clinic religious authenticity."

"Let me guess. Saint Joseph."

"Yes, exactly! How did you know? I wanted to buy the large Madonna, but he wouldn't sell it to me. Anyway, as I walked around the shop looking at the extraordinary number of religious objects, I noticed that there was something odd about the building itself."

Halloran said nothing and waited for her to continue.

"Oh, this is going to sound crazy," she said.

"Go ahead."

"Between the showroom and the workshop there appears to be several feet of unused space. Behind a wall, if you know what I mean."

"Like a storeroom?"

"It could be. But why would you need a storeroom when there is that huge workroom in the back?" she asked.

"A corridor? A walled-up staircase?"

"More like a hiding place."

"Interesting."

"I could be imagining it, but as I was looking at the wall where it didn't quite meet the adjacent wall in a flush manner, the owner was watching me intently. I managed to deflect his interest by looking at a hymnal of some kind."

"Ah, so you *are* thinking of coming back to the real religion," he teased.

"Honestly, Brendan, I don't think it is appropriate to be sacrilegious."

He laughed. "I'm not! It's just that you Anglicans started out at the spot where we were already at and then decided to make something new."

"You're diverting me from the reason I called you. Something is not right with Mr. Rinaldi and his shop. He seems very skittish."

"I can imagine he is after what happened to his son."

"Are you any closer to finding out who might have done it?"

"Leads in every direction, but I have a feeling people are trying to divert my attention. I am hoping you are not one of them."

"Of course not! I'm trying to help. Even if you don't want me to."

He paused. "There is a way you can help me. I need to make a visit to the Oasis, and it would look better if you were to go with me."

"Look better? What does that mean?"

"Even if I'm in civilian clothes, people might get suspicious if I'm not with a date."

"So, are you asking me out on a date?"

"I suppose I am."

"I suppose I'll accept. Surely not tonight. It's Sunday."

"How about tomorrow night? Monday."

"I have to get up early for the clinic opening on Tuesday."

"I guess you are going to make me go through the days of the week. What about Tuesday evening in celebration of your achievement."

"That will be fine. But you'll have to pick me up at my house. No more sneaking down the back stairs for me."

"Sounds perfect. See you then."

Amanda hung up the phone feeling rather smug. Her sister wasn't the only one who had men interested in her.

## Chapter 14

Monday morning got off to a wild start with an ice storm that threatened to shut down traffic and certainly gave Amanda pause as she looked out her bedroom window. The trees in the back garden, bare since fall, had been covered in water from a late-night storm before being encased in ice as the temperature dropped. It was a glittering sight, but she knew her mother would be distraught about the possible damage to her plants. Amanda was more concerned about how to let her parents know she was going out on a date with a policeman. Well, detective, if that made any difference.

The breakfast room on the floor below faced the garden and just as she suspected, her mother was looking out at sparkling branches and only seeing possible destruction.

"I hope they're not severely damaged," she said.

"They've been here longer than we have, you know. I'm sure they've seen worse," Mr. Burnside said from behind his newspaper. He put it down for a moment to distract his wife.

"Margaret, you said that Louisa called yesterday, and everything sounded fine. Did she say what she is doing, exactly?"

"A lot of social things," Amanda said, coming into the room. "Flitting about with tea dances and such." She sat down and poured coffee for herself. "Visiting plantations and pretending to be a Southern belle."

He scowled. "I thought there were going to be beach trips or something."

"Evidently not. Maybe it's still too chilly, or they don't have beaches nearby. She spoke mostly of social events."

"I hope she doesn't come back with expectations of living the high life that she is experiencing there," her mother said.

"Her hostess is trying to show her the most glamorous parts of Charleston, just as you would show a visitor the best of Boston. That's not real life for anyone," Amanda said.

Her father sighed. "I'm glad you have a head on your shoulders."

"I'd look pretty silly without one, don't you think?"

Mr. Burnside chuckled and resumed reading.

"Oh, where is breakfast?" Mrs. Burnside asked.

"Is Cook still in a tizzy?" Amanda asked softly.

"I'm afraid so. I don't know why she thinks things will go awry without Nora. Not that she wasn't an excellent worker. But it's Mary whose nose is out of joint, thinking she'll have twice the work for the same pay."

They were silenced by Mary coming through the swinging door to the kitchen with a platter of sausages and another of French toast.

"Good morning, Ma'am, Sir, Miss," she said perfunctorily before leaving.

When the door had swung closed, Amanda spoke. "I didn't tell you, but I talked to a young girl to whom I was introduced last week. I let her know that you were looking for someone and thought I'd give you her number."

"What?" Mrs. Burnside said. She wasn't used to making these arrangements herself.

"I can set up an informal interview for you and be present as well if that's more comfortable. She seems to be personable, a hard worker and anxious to have a job of her own instead of working for her parents. Not that she minds working for them. But another income in the family would be welcome, as you can imagine."

"Has she worked in a house before?'

"Probably not. And I'm not sure that once she knows the duties and the salary that she will want to take it. But it's a step forward, isn't it? We don't want long faces all day." Here Amanda nodded her head toward the kitchen, where usually murmurings of conversation could be heard but today was ominously silent.

"I suppose," her mother said, the crease between her brows appearing again.

"I need to go to the hospital this morning and make sure everything is ready for the clinic opening tomorrow. But I can be back this afternoon if you wish to interview her."

"That would be helpful. What is her name?"

"Simona Catalano."

"Oh," her mother observed.

"I think you'll be surprised," Amanda said, trying not to confront her mother's assumptions head on.

"I don't know if you should take the car out in these conditions," her mother said.

"Look, the ice is melting already," Mr. Burnside said. "Amanda, if you don't want to drive, I can drop you off."

"I don't think it will be too slick. I'll need the car to bring the potential maid in for an interview." She patted the hand of her mother, who worried so much about things. And then she realized she ought to hold off informing them about the date until a bit later in the day. Or perhaps the next day.

THINGS at the hospital were somewhat disrupted by the ice storm, with employees calling in about their inability to get to work and others coming in late. Amanda found the roads a bit slick, but by the time she encountered the heavier traffic, the roads were slushy rather than treacherous. Her first task was to call Mr. De Luca at the Sons of Italy Hall to inquire if there was anything else to be done for Tuesday. He picked up the phone immediately, which led her to wonder if he had a job of any kind; she had originally assumed that this was a part-time volunteer endeavor on his part but, as her interactions with him increased, it appeared he spent all his time there. Perhaps the members paid dues and that might be what sustained his efforts as he didn't appear old enough to be retired.

"Ah, Miss Burnside. How kind of you to call. We seem to be ready for tomorrow. The janitor will move the furniture into place late this afternoon. All that will be lacking are the doctors and nurses and someone to act as receptionist."

Amanda had delegated that task to Miss Bailey, with Mr. Barlow's approval, although she knew she had to get someone else for the long term.

"What time shall we be there tomorrow?" she asked.

"We expect people at nine o'clock so I would say if you're here at eight that should be enough time to set up whatever other equipment you'll be bringing."

Amanda had a list of those additional things gathered from the medical floor and stashed away. She even thought of securing an autoclave so they would not have to bring back dirty instruments to the hospital, although they would certainly be sterilized again.

"Very good, we'll see you tomorrow." She let her mind run over a likely scenario of women lining up inside the building, Miss Bailey taking their names and getting a brief description of the medical issue at hand. She assumed that Fred would be the one to prioritize the patients based on the seriousness of the situation, but if it were a real emergency, they ought to proceed to the hospital. Amanda hoped that someone wasn't going to come in with a life-threatening condition. In that case, they would have to play it by ear.

About an hour into her workday, Mr. Barlow came to her office and informed her that Miss Bailey wouldn't be in that day or much of the week as she had influenza.

"I'm sorry to hear that as it leaves you strapped," she said to him. "Me, as well. I guess I'll have to play receptionist tomorrow."

"If the next few weeks turn out to be a positive trial run, you'll have to get someone to take on those duties on a permanent basis," he reminded her.

"Perhaps we can get a student nurse to do it since it doesn't require medical skills per se. I'd hate to ask a qualified nurse to use her time in that way. At least a student might benefit from getting used to what sorts of cases might present themselves," she said.

She took a few minutes to call home and see if her mother had contacted Simona and learned that they had set up a meeting for early afternoon and Amanda was to pick her up and bring her to Beacon Hill for that purpose. She sighed, knowing that it would put a dent in her workday, but realized that having her mother's worries assuaged was of great importance to the entire household.

About two o'clock, when the restaurant's lunch business had quieted down, Amanda set out for the North End to pick up the young girl. Even opening the front door to the enclosed foyer brought the enticing smells of baked bread and mouthwatering food. Simona was seated, folding napkins, and jumped up as Amanda came in, looking flustered.

"Am I dressed appropriately?" she asked.

"Of course. You're in day clothes. My mother would expect nothing more at this stage. If you come to an agreement, we do have uniforms."

"Oh," Simona responded, not having thought of that aspect. She turned and waved to her mother, who was looking through the passage into the kitchen, took her coat and hat from the nearby chair and followed Amanda out to the street.

"Now, don't be nervous, my mother won't bite."

That got a short laugh in response, but for most of the trip to Beacon Hill, Amanda did all the talking, pointing out landmarks and chatting about her family. Simona sat with her hands in her lap, her large green eyes looking straight ahead.

Amanda brought her into the sitting room where her mother sat, looking almost as nervous as the young girl, made the introductions and said she would be in the kitchen until they were done. She wanted a cup of tea, and it was also the warmest room in the house. She could be sure to encounter Cook and perhaps Mary and make them at ease that someone else might be coming on soon to lighten their workload.

"Has she had this kind of job before?" Mary asked as Cook filled the kettle.

"I'm not sure. But I know she's the only girl in the family, so you can be sure she's done her share of housework. She just graduated high school in December and has been helping at her family's restaurant."

"She's not going to be cooking that Eye-talian food, is she?" Cook asked, sitting down at the butcher block table with the other two women.

"I'm sure not. Her mother is the chef in the restaurant, her father runs things, and she has been seating people and serving the food. Other things, too, but I made it clear that cooking wouldn't be part of the job."

"Good." Cook nodded at Mary.

"Since I've been here longer, I think that your mother ought to give me the easier part of the tasks. I have a terrible time with lifting the heavy things. My back tends to ache by the end of the day," Mary said.

"I think you ought to talk to Mother about that," Amanda said, with a smile, but having no intention of getting involved any further in the running of the household. She could see that Mary had already taken it into her head that Simona was going to be her pet and realized there was no way she could dissuade her from that notion. Instead, she made her own tea and asked them questions about their families, which were large, and it took quite some time to hear the details as well as keep track of who was who.

Mrs. Burnside popped her head through the door to the kitchen and asked Amanda to join her in the sitting room. She got up, thanked Cook for the tea and conversation, followed her mother back to the sitting room and sat down.

"We've had a nice talk and I believe Simona will be a helpful addition to the household."

"That's good," Amanda said and could see the young woman was pleased as well.

"I've given her the outline of what is expected, the days off, the salary and if I've forgotten anything, I'll fill her in on it later. So, we'll see you tomorrow, then?"

"I just have to get my parents' final approval."

"Oh," Mrs. Burnside said, not having thought that would be necessary.

"I'm sure they'll say yes, Ma'am. Thank you." Simona stood and shook Mrs. Burnside's hand vigorously. "I will try my best."

"Well then, let's take you back home, shall we?" Amanda said and led the new maid out the front door to the car parked in the street.

"Your mother is ever so nice," Simona said.

"She's not the one you'll have to win over."

"You mean Cook and Mary. I know how to do that. I've worked with some difficult people in the past. Not that they will be difficult," she hastened to add.

Amanda signaled and pulled out into the deserted street.

"Who?"

"Customers. Neighbors. People in the North End want to know everyone's business and keep tabs on where you are going, what you are wearing and report back to the parents. It is very annoying. 'Simona had makeup on yesterday,' one of them said."

"That is petty."

"It will be a relief to get away from some of that." She looked around as they drove past the staid homes. "What a beautiful neighborhood."

"Yes, it is."

"The thing that troubles me is the intense politics of the menfolk. Some are constantly pressuring my father to take one side or another in political issues."

"Like who is running for Mayor?"

"More than that. National politics, I guess you could call it. Whether Italians should support Mussolini and the Fascist League of America or steer clear of them entirely. I mean, they love their former homeland, but they are Americans now and shouldn't want to get involved in all that."

"I can imagine. The world had enough of such things after the Great War. To think that regional politics evolved into such a global event," Amanda said, thinking of her uncle, who had served and suffered lung damage as a result.

"And some of these men come into the restaurant and pester me. Make advances toward me and I know it is just to get to my father. I'll be glad to leave that behind. Thank you, Miss Burnside. I think you have done me a great favor."

## Chapter 15

Amanda was not used to having to wake up so early, but she had promised Salvatore De Luca that she would be there by eight. No light outside, she wondered how some working people managed to get up in the dark and come home in the gloom in the early evening. She was beginning to envy Louisa even more where the difference in latitude surely meant more sunlight at the beginning and end of the day.

She made her own breakfast as Cook had not come in yet and scurried through the frigid house to get herself dressed warmly enough to sit in the chilly Sons of Italy basement all day. She eyed the lap blanket on the end of the bed and decided she would take it with her and perhaps keep her coat on, as surely the women who came in would do the same.

The only traffic on the streets were milkmen, trucks and delivery vehicles making the rounds before the commuter traffic began and, although crowded, the drivers made haste to get their work done. When she approached the building, she was surprised to see several women with their children standing outside the front doors and asked them if they were there for the clinic.

"Yes, Miss," the first in line said.

"Is the door locked?" she asked and tugged on it to find it open.

"Come in," Amanda said, and they shyly entered, only to be confronted by the janitor.

"Mr. De Luca said the clinic opens at nine o'clock," he said, his eyebrows drawn together against the challenge to his authority.

"We can't let them wait outside in the cold with children who may be sick," she countered and led the way down the stairs to the basement, looking for the light switches on the wall and bringing illumination to the space. The janitor at least had the heat turned on and it wasn't the icebox she imagined it might be, leaving her feeling a bit silly for having brought a blanket.

The women stood, not knowing what to do, but she motioned them to the chairs that had been set up in rows. Taking a receipt book out of her carryall that allowed for a carbon copy between pages, she approached the first woman and asked her name. It was only then that she realized that she didn't know about the conventions of Italian spelling and had to show the woman what she was writing, only to have it corrected. The name Paglia was spelled very differently from how it was pronounced. Good thing she was writing in pencil. Then she asked the reason she had come in with her son and jotted down, 'sore throat.' On to the next woman. When she had finished with the three women and left them chatting with each other, she moved the makeshift reception desk from the middle of the room toward the entrance to the basement. It seemed more welcoming to her, less like approaching a tribunal, and she could catch anyone who tried to slip in without registering.

As she settled herself, she was pleased that the flyers and word of mouth had been successful enough to bring these early birds. But she wasn't prepared for what turned out to be a constant stream of women coming down the stairs, giving their names and taking their places in the congregation of chairs. By the time Fred, the resident and two nurses appeared a short time later, there were already almost fifteen families represented and the noise level rose as the women chatted with each other and the children who were well enough explored the room and were shooed off by the janitor when they passed a certain invisible boundary.

Fred's eyebrows rose as he contemplated the volume of potential patients and set the nurses to work getting some testing equipment into the adjacent kitchen. No sooner had one nurse put out the autoclave and instruments than a woman bustled into the basement with several shopping bags and, seeing the activity, stopped dead in her tracks.

"What's going on here?"

"It's the new children's clinic. Tuesday and Wednesday each week."

"Nobody told me!" she said loudly.

"Who are you?" Amanda said politely.

"I'm from the health department. I'm here to give a class in nutrition."

Amanda stood up and motioned to the janitor, who was sulkily standing guard across the room. He came over to them with a scowl on his face.

"I'm supposed to do a nutrition class here today. Where is Mr. De Luca?"

"I'll go get him," the janitor replied and made his way slowly up the stairs.

"I can't believe there has been a mix-up," the woman said.

"I'm Amanda Burnside. I work with Mercy Hospital, which has arranged to have an additional clinic in the neighborhood so families wouldn't have to travel so far for treatment."

The woman put her shopping bags down and held out her hand. "Genevieve Butler." She sighed. "I don't know how this is going to work."

"I'm sure there is room for both activities," Amanda said.

After some minutes, De Luca came down the stairs by himself, all smiles, and explained that the janitor must have misunderstood. "We can put your table and easel over in that corner, Miss Butler. There are enough chairs so that we can move some over to your demonstration area. See?" he asked, picking up a few chairs and positioning them facing a table in the back.

She was not pleased at having second position and set her mouth tightly. "It's going to be chaos in here as I try to explain the 'Principles of Nutrition for Young Children' to these ladies amid the racket of these children tearing around."

Amanda surveyed the children and the adults seated in the room and didn't think any of them looked malnourished and wondered why they needed instruction in that topic. Against her better judgment, she asked Miss Butler to explain why she was there.

The other woman pulled her aside and said in a forceful whisper. "Haven't you seen what these people eat?" She looked around to see if anyone could overhear her. "Spaghetti and all kinds of noodles and bread. Pure starch! Hardly any meat or chops of any sort. I don't know where they get their protein. And very little milk or dairy products. No butter to speak of but all that olive oil!"

"I haven't eaten in peoples' homes, just in restaurants, but the food seemed healthy and delicious," Amanda offered.

"Yes, but that's not your everyday diet. Haven't you noticed that their children are smaller than American children?"

"Now that you mention it, yes. But the men and women are shorter, too. I must seem like a giant to them," Amanda laughed.

Miss Butler was not amused. "They'll get a lot of useful information from this demonstration, and they can begin to buy some of our healthy American food products instead of all these imported canned goods they seem to favor."

At this point, Amanda wondered who had really sponsored this woman's talk. Was it about making sure there were healthy children or that they were buying enough from America's farmers?

More women were coming into the room and Amanda excused herself. She also looked at her watch and, although it was only eight forty-five, the doctors and nurses were ready, so it seemed reasonable that they should start. She gave the nurse the yellow copy of the first patient's name and once called out, the woman and her son stepped forward and behind one of the privacy panels to be examined by Fred or the resident.

The nurse called out the second name, "Morelli."

The room went instantly silent. The nurse was baffled, then adjusted her glasses and said, "Excuse me, Moretti."

There was a titter of laughter through the room and a woman came up to the nurse and said in her face, "Moretti," with emphasis on the last syllable. Her face was in a snarl, and Amanda could see the gold-rimmed front tooth and the set of her shoulders. Then the woman turned to the other women and said something in Italian accompanied by a shrug that made them all laugh.

When she had gone ahead, the nurse said to Amanda, "What did I do wrong?"

"Nothing. It's just that Morelli is the big man in this neighborhood. And she clearly is not his wife or relation."

The nurse looked puzzled.

Amanda mouthed the word, "Gangster."

The nurse's eyes widened, and she forced a smile. "Pardon me," she said and followed the patient in to see the resident. Fred poked his head out from behind an adjacent privacy screen and, seeing the increasing crowd, looked over at Amanda, scowled and disappeared.

"*That's the thanks I get for setting this up,*" she thought and was disturbed by his increasing coldness toward her. He was dating Valerie now, someone much more compliant who would love being the stay-at-home wife of a prominent doctor.

Her eyes went to the table in the corner where Miss Butler was speaking to a group of six women, holding up what looked like papier-mâché fruits, vegetables, eggs, meat and an empty bottle of milk for illustration. The other women waiting for medical attention glanced over from time to time wondering what was going on, and Miss Butler, noticing their interest, had flyers at the ready for an upcoming demonstration.

Toward noon no newcomers appeared, which didn't mean that they might not swarm in after lunch. Amanda decided it was a good time for her to ask one of the nurses to take over the reception desk while she went out for a bite to eat and to assure Mr. and Mrs. Catalano that Simona was in good hands. It wouldn't hurt that she could get a hot bowl of minestrone or lentil soup, as well.

Bundled against the cold, she scurried down the street past a man selling boots and shoes from a pushcart with several women looking over the goods and murmuring to each other. How different from her experience shopping. Were these women going to try on the shoes right there in the street or hope for the best in terms of fit and stuff the toes with tissue if they were too big? When she bought shoes, she sat in a comfortable chair in a store, the clerk brought over several styles, she was shoehorned into a pair and able to walk around on the carpet to see how they felt. Angled mirrors at floor level provided a reflection, and she could take her time and ease at deciding which pair to buy. More pushcarts up the street had men's shirts and sweaters for sale, hawked by a man shouting something in Italian.

There were no fruits or vegetables to be seen out in the street except potatoes and cabbages that could withstand the cold.

As usual, Catalano's restaurant was redolent of the scents of warm bread and hearty dishes, and she was welcomed by Mr. Catalano with open arms.

"We thank you for arranging the job for Simona," he said, then grasping her hands. "And you are so cold! Here, let me take your coat," which he did, hanging it on the coatrack and then showing her to one of the remaining empty seats.

"I see business is good," she said.

"Better all the time."

"May I have some very hot coffee, first? And then you can tell me what the Signora has for lunch today." He moved quickly to the kitchen, returning with a steaming cup and a pitcher of milk.

"She has a special treat today. Have you ever had braciole?"

"Not only have I not had it, I also don't know what it is." She laughed and took a sip of the coffee, instantly feeling a bit warmer. There were three men seated at the other side of the room and the larger of the three, dressed in an expensive three-piece suit was looking at her. She tried to place him—perhaps someone who was at the ribbon cutting. But then she remembered they had passed on the street one day and he had tipped his hat. At that time, she had noticed him but, of course, did not acknowledge the courtesy since she didn't know who he was.

"It is a special cut of beef stuffed and rolled up," here Mr. Catalano motioned with his hands. "With spinach and cheese and a fragrant tomato sauce."

"I'm sold," she said, having enjoyed his wife's pungent sauce before, nothing like the bland red stuff that Cook used to top stuffed cabbage, one of her most unfavorite creations.

She continued to sip the coffee, sensing the eyes of the man on her, something that she thought was quite bold, but rather than give him an icy stare back, she ignored the attention and took a piece of paper and her fountain pen out of her handbag and began jotting down some notes about how the layout of the clinic had worked and in what way it could be improved. She was engrossed in her work but heard the three men complimenting Mr. Catalano on his wife's cooking before they made their exit, purposefully coming by her table. She didn't look up but knew the man had looked down at her and she saw his hand with a pinky ring. He wore cologne, an unusual thing for the men that she knew. They were supposed to have the scent of pipe smoke, cigars, leather and sometimes sandalwood soap. But cologne? That was strange.

The men put on their coats and left, letting a draft of cold air in despite the enclosed foyer. She gave a shiver and looked up to see Mr. Catalano carrying her plate of food as if it were a prized possession.

"It does look good."

He nodded and before he turned away, she asked, "Who was that man who kept looking in my direction?"

His face fell and he lowered his voice. "That was Mr. Morelli."

"Oh," she said. He didn't look very threatening in real life.

"And some bread," he added, putting a small basket down in front of her. "He always comes in for my wife's braciole. He even once told her that he'd like her to come be his chef and the poor woman was so startled that she couldn't answer him. It turned out he was just teasing her because he already has a chef and said that his wife would be jealous if there were a woman in the kitchen." He smiled without much enthusiasm.

Amanda could not imagine working for a gangster—if that accurately described who he was or what he did. He wasn't tearing around in a car, shooting a Tommy gun from the running boards like in the movies she had seen. Maybe he was just an influential man in the community who people respected because he had become wealthy. Doing what, she wondered. Maybe she ought not refer to him as a gangster. She would have to ask Halloran what sort of 'business' the man might be in. She stopped mid-bite to remember that they were going to the Oasis that evening and she hadn't yet told her parents about it. Amanda put that part from her mind for a moment to consider if she had time to wash her hair and what dress she would filch from her sister's closet. She knew Louisa had packed a few evening things but didn't dare take some of the more low-cut numbers that might scandalize her hostess.

"You must be enjoying your lunch, judging from the cat that got the cream look on your face," a voice at her elbow said.

She looked up to see Halloran standing there, still in his hat and coat.

"You could say hello," he said with that teasing twinkle in his eye.

"Yes, hello. Have you eaten yet?"

"No," he answered. "I'm not sure if that was an invitation or just an inquiry."

"Well, sit down. Mrs. Catalano has outdone herself if that's possible."

He returned to the coat rack, hung up his hat and coat and returned to her table.

"I've only just begun," she said.

The owner came over to the table, greeted Halloran and asked if he would like the braciole.

"Of course! It's Tuesday, isn't it?" He rubbed his cold hands together. "I went by the clinic to see how things were going and they said you had gone out to lunch. I figured you weren't at the hot dog stand, stamping your feet to keep them warm."

"Absolutely not! Who would eat out of doors in this weather unless they needed to? Besides, I didn't know there was a hot dog stand around."

"Those of us who often have to eat on the run know these things." His plate of food was placed before him almost immediately. "Ah, one of my favorites."

"It's very tasty but I can't make out all the ingredients. By the way, you just missed Mr. Morelli."

Halloran looked up quickly at her face, trying to read the expression.

"He was in here eating with two of his friends."

"I believe they are called henchmen, lieutenants or minions. How do you know who it was?"

"Mr. Catalano told me after they left. Mr. Morelli kept looking over at my table and I asked afterward who he was."

"He can come across as charming, but don't be fooled. He's as lethal as a cobra and twice as fast. Try not to pay any attention to him. And I'd advise you to forget that you even met him."

# Chapter 16

They finished their meal in a cordial tone but beneath her polite demeanor, Amanda was annoyed at Halloran's presumption to tell her of whom she should be wary. After all, she felt she could take care of herself in social situations and the likelihood that she should encounter the man again outside of a crowded restaurant was miniscule. They parted pleasantly enough with the agreement that he would pick her up at eight o'clock. He went off in one direction and she in the other to witness the last hours of the clinic that was due to end at three o'clock.

Amanda was pleased to note that there were only a handful of women left and no new ones had arrived in the basement room. Fred came out from the kitchen, wiping his hands after having washed them, and greeted her with a tight smile.

"Is everything going well?" she asked him.

"Quite a show today."

"What do you mean?" She was anxious that something untoward had occurred during her lunch break.

"The sheer number of patients is unlike anything I've seen, even at the main clinic."

"Well, it's the first of its kind."

"I realize we may need to have tetanus vaccine on hand, too. I treated a good many cuts and abrasions."

"Did you encounter any serious cases?"

"Not really. One child might have had some vision problems and I suggested they see an eye doctor. Ringworm, head lice and a few cases where the child was averse to soap and water. In those situations, a stern talking to may have changed the young lad's mind about bathing."

"I don't know what the living conditions are for these families, if they even have bathtubs readily available or hot water," Amanda said.

"Louisa was studying social work. What does she have to say about that?"

"The truth is, she was only pretending. In reality, she was studying social activities at my parents' expense."

Fred looked shocked. "Nothing improper, I hope."

"No, just a boyfriend and nightclubs. She has been sent away for a while."

"To a sanatorium?" Fred asked.

Amanda laughed. "Her punishment is quite mild. She's in Charleston with a friend's family and having the time of her life."

Fred scowled.

She thought it odd that he was so conservative in some ways, yet had a very unconventional mother who wrote steamy romance novels and a sister who was a habitué of nightclubs. Perhaps his staid attitude was in reaction to having such relatives, she thought, and then realized it was no longer any of her concern.

The afternoon wound down and the janitor began taking some of the partitions away to stack in a nearby storeroom and folding up the metal chairs to place them in a corner. Amanda thought this was a wasted effort since the clinic would resume in the morning, but then she saw that he was putting up tables for some evening event. This building seemed to serve a multitude of needs for the community.

The doctors and nurses packed up well before three while Amanda reviewed the receipt booklet that she had used to check in the patients. It looked like there had been more than sixty, which would have been a record number for the parent clinic. Perhaps because it was opening day, there was a rush to deal with untreated health issues. Or maybe this was an indicator of the level of traffic that they could expect here, the neighborhood being so populous.

A RELAXING BATH with a hair wash in the quiet house was her first action upon getting home, knowing that both parents were likely not to return for a few hours. She set in the clips that produced waves in her light brown hair and clothed in a bathrobe, decided to raid her sister's closet for a fetching gown for the evening.

Either Louisa had left her room fairly neat, or Mary or Simona had tidied up since she left. The contents of the closet were another matter. Some of the dresses were half off their hangers, almost as if she had yanked them and not replaced them carefully. Amanda did so, rehanging each dress as she silently scolded her sister, who tended to be careless. Then she opened the closet door wider to have more light. She hadn't expected there to be so many dresses considering Louisa must have taken some with her. Then again, if she were out several times a week, she couldn't be seen in the same frock night after night.

"Wore that already," Amanda said, pushing the mauve dress to the left, "I look awful in green," again moving it to the left. "Ah, that's interesting." It was deep blue with a sweetheart neckline, somewhat sedate for a nightclub, but entirely appropriate to be wearing in front of her parents when Halloran picked her up. Her stomach tightened at the thought of their reaction since she hadn't mentioned it to them yet. She would wait until dinner was in full swing with the maids coming and going so there would be no opportunity for an obvious reaction. If Louisa could date a nightclub owner, then an Irish detective ought not faze them. Or would it?

She heard a tap on the door and her mother pushed it open further.

"You gave me a start!" Mrs. Burnside said.

"Me, too!" Amanda said. "I'm raiding Louisa's closet for something suitable to wear tonight."

"I should think you have enough clothing," her mother said.

Still with her head in the closet, Amanda replied, "I'm going out to a club tonight so I can't very well wear a woolen jumper." She waited for some kind of response but heard nothing.

"What do you think of this?" she asked as she pulled the navy dress out. "High neckline, long sleeves. It should keep me warm." She neglected to add that the back was cut low.

Her mother stammered. "I suppose that's what you young girls do these days instead of going to a friend's house for the evening."

"These clubs always have live music, which is much more fun that having someone stationed at the player changing the records."

"I see. Will you be here for dinner?"

"Oh, yes. We're going out about eight o'clock." Amanda was still perusing Louisa's evening gown collection and not looking at her mother.

"Who are you going with?"

"Brendan. I think you met him last year at the Valentine Ball."

"There were so many young men there, I didn't catch all their names."

"You'll probably recognize him when he gets here."

"Very well, I'd better see how things are progressing downstairs. That Simona is a very bright girl. A hard worker and eager to please. And Mary's nose is not at all out of joint having someone new come in."

Amanda pulled her head out of the closet. "I'm glad to hear it."

Her mother pointed at Amanda's head.

She answered, "These things? It will give a bit of wave to my hair."

"I see," her mother said, leaving the room.

Amanda was relieved that her mother was palmed off so easily and wondered if she would recognize Halloran. She then wondered if she had shoes that would work with the dress. She could always wear her black pumps, but she bet that Louisa had some navy ones somewhere in the closet.

Several pairs were lined up on the floor but there were stacks of shoe boxes at the back, unfortunately none of them labeled. She pulled out one after the other and found that she was looking at summer sandals and tennis shoes. She kept digging and saw a glittery pair of silver heels but decided they might distract from the impact of the dress. Stack number two: red shoes, saddle shoes, brogans and black pumps. Stack number three: a lightweight box, not shoes, but piles of folded papers, notes of some kind. Opening one she saw that it was a handwritten receipt for a loan with the bold letters, IOU for two hundred dollars with a scribbled signature at the bottom. The paper it was written on was stationery with Rob Worley's name at the top.

Amanda sat on the bed and methodically went through the stack, some with the same illegible signature, others more easily decipherable although she didn't recognize any of the names. There must have been several thousand dollars' worth of personal loans outstanding. No need to ask what this precious information was doing at the bottom of a stack of shoe boxes in Louisa's closet. Rob would have been a fool to keep them in his own office or home for fear they would be stolen. Even a safe could be stolen or blown open. But he could at least have had the decency to open a safety deposit box and not involve her sister in his shady business dealings.

She looked out the window and shook her head. Was her sister becoming a gangster's moll? Who even thought up that term? Rob wasn't really a gangster, was he? Whatever he was, he was sitting on quite a lot of accounts receivable, which put him in a dangerous position if these folks couldn't or wouldn't pay up. And Louisa by extension was in danger as well. If anyone knew what was in the bottom of her closet, that is. The next time she called they would have to have a quiet talk about things.

Dinner was unremarkable and Amanda mentioned that she was going out that evening although her father didn't seem to take note of it. Her mother cleared her throat and her father looked up.

"Am I supposed to be remarking on something? Such as, your hair looks very à la mode?"

"Thank you, Daddy, I didn't think you would notice."

"Do I know the young man?"

"I believe you have met before."

There was a pause. "And his name?"

"Brendan. Halloran."

There was the sound of cutlery on the dishes.

"Hm," her father said.

Amanda turned the conversation to what was puzzling her. "Daddy, one thing that was brought to my attention being in the North End is that people there feel strongly about their ties to their homeland."

"That's only natural. Many of them have only been here one generation or less."

"I don't mean customs and food; I mean the political situation in Italy. I can see from the newsreels that the current leader is causing quite a stir. Some people here think he is bringing order and others are afraid that he has become a dictator."

"That's a good observation. You must remember that Italy was once a collection of city-states and regions. The geography itself tends to support it. People may speak Italian but there are dialects, as well. It isn't like America where you might have some trouble understanding a person from Alabama, for example, but that's an accent, not a dialect or an entirely different language. The country was only unified in 1870. That was in my father's lifetime. I'll bet you Italians still identify themselves based on region."

"Well, we're only a hundred years older," Amanda observed.

"Yes, but those people have lived in the same cities, villages and hill towns for centuries. The earliest our forebears came was in the 1600s. Many of them have moved extensively since then. We all speak the same language although when I hear some of the folks on the street these days, I do wonder."

Amanda consulted her watch. "I'd better get ready," she said, excusing herself from the table, not noticing the looks her parents were exchanging as she left.

Louisa's dress fit well although a tad short, but not notice-
ably so. Amanda powdered her nose, dabbed a bit of
rouge, applied lipstick and wondered if she should pilfer
Louisa's mascara as well. Why not? It was a little red box
with a tiny brush that had to be wet to activate the square
of pigment. She went to the bathroom for water and better
light. At first, she didn't think it would make a difference
but was pleasantly surprised that between the eye makeup
and the navy dress her blue eyes were more noticeable. She
was very pleased with herself and dabbed perfume on her
wrists and behind her ears. The doorbell rang and she took
a deep breath to go down the stairs.

Brendan looked elegant and sophisticated in his evening
clothes, white silk scarf and overcoat, his hat held in his
hands as he shook Mr. Burnside's hand and introduced
himself.

"Please, come in," her father said, ushering him to a chair
in the sitting room.

Amanda chose that moment to come slowly down the
stairs, noting that Brendan was taking in her slim figure
and the lovely dress. She had already slung an evening coat
over her shoulders not only to disguise the low-cut back but
also to hasten their exit lest her father ask him too many
questions.

Mrs. Burnside appeared. "Can I get you some coffee?"

Brendan stood up. "Thank you, no. We're meeting some
people and wouldn't want to keep them waiting."

Good one, thought Amanda.

"It was a pleasure to meet you. I'll be sure to get Amanda
back early. I know she's had a long day."

He helped her fully into her coat, thanked Mr. Burnside again and ushered her out the door.

"That is a very becoming dress," he said, turning his eyes on her as they got to the car.

"I snitched it from Louisa's closet. You'll never believe what you can find in there."

# Chapter 17

"All went well at the end of the clinic?" Brendan asked.

"It was very busy, and I think Fred and the resident were exhausted by the end of it. I don't think they even took a break for lunch. I should feel guilty about that."

"You have proven your point that providing basic care to areas outside the precincts of Mercy Hospital is needed and welcomed."

"Yes, I guess you're right." Amanda smiled, relishing her success. "We're open for business again tomorrow. I wonder if there will be as large a crowd." She glanced out the window at the passing scene as they headed toward the Oasis. It was funny to think that just a few months ago she had never been in such a place and now she looked forward to going. She was beginning to see its allure for Louisa.

A different doorman from the one she had seen previously approached their car when they drove up. He was wearing the same faux Mideastern costume as the other one: a spangled vest over a billowing white shirt, full pants that were gathered at the ankles and an enormous, gilded turban with a blue stone in front. She glanced down at his shoes which had pointed, curved tips and wondered how that large, muscled man, who might also serve as a bouncer, felt about wearing such a ridiculous costume. They probably paid him well and it was certain nobody was going to point a finger and laugh in his face.

He opened the door for her, then went to the driver's side and took the keys from Brendan to park the car. Another similarly dressed doorman took his place outside the entrance, waiting for the next vehicle. The front door was opened, providing a welcome gust of warm air from the interior.

"That feels good after the freezing weather outside, but I don't see how you men can be comfortable in all those clothes," she said.

"One of the peculiar aspects of evening clothes. Men have on so many layers and women practically none." They checked their outer wear with a young woman with marcel waves at the stand just inside the door.

"Oh, look, there's Caroline and José," Amanda said and walked toward their table. There was the slightest lift of a tweezed eyebrow as Caroline surveyed Amanda's escort although she had met him previously.

"How nice to see you again," she said, holding her hand out as if it were to be kissed.

"Are you here most nights?" Amanda asked.

"Well, it's his work, after all."

"And how is business?" Brendan asked, surveying the room that was not quite full but it was still early.

"Come sit down," Caroline said and called to her husband, who had his back turned, speaking to another man. He excused himself and greeted them effusively.

"I'm so glad you've come back. Especially after that unpleasantness I heard took place."

"Just part of the game, I guess," Brendan said, pulling out a chair for Amanda.

José snapped his fingers, and a waiter came hurriedly up and was spoken to in such low tones that Amanda couldn't hear what was said.

"Aren't you going to ask me how my brother is?" Caroline asked.

"I don't need to. I was with him most of the day at the temporary clinic in the North End. It was very busy so I'm sure he is tired."

"Fred? Never. He has incredible stamina. I think all doctors need to have that. Me? I could never work those hours, get up at the crack of dawn and do it all over again. And deliver babies in the middle of the night!" She shuddered. "And where is Louisa?" she asked although Amanda was certain she knew.

"Visiting some friends in South Carolina."

"How exotic. I've never been south of the Mason-Dixon line except by boat with José's family. We went directly from New York to Cuba. That was exciting."

José smiled at his wife. "It's a wonderful country. Beautiful with acres and acres of sugar fields. For the rum, you know."

"And they have casinos and nightclubs where they are allowed to serve alcohol, unlike this Puritan country," Caroline added, adjusting a glittering earring as Amanda wondered if they were diamond or rhinestone.

"It looks like you all are trying your best to change all that," Brendan said. He looked up as Rob Worley came into view in a white dinner jacket, his smile dazzling against his tan skin. Not for the first time did Amanda wonder how he managed to look as if he had just returned from a tropical vacation while most Bostonians were pasty-faced.

"Hello," he said to Amanda, bending to kiss her cheek. He shook Brendan's hand firmly.

"How nice of you to visit this evening."

"No surprises in store?" Brendan asked.

Rob chuckled. "The games grown men play."

"The Chief is already here," Caroline said, garnering a frown from Rob. "In one of the private rooms with all kinds of important men." She took a cigarette out of her purse and held it up for José to light.

Brendan gave a quizzical glance at Rob.

"Nothing to do with us. Surely, you've heard about some political unrest in the North End?"

"It's always there. What's new now?"

"I'm not sure, but I believe we're about to find out." He looked up as Henry Rogers emerged from one of the private rooms and headed their way.

"Say," said Henry as he recognized Amanda. He then looked at Brendan, whom he didn't recognize at first, seeing him out of the usual context. "I guess this is the place to be."

"Sit down," Brendan said, eager to get the lowdown. "What's the confab all about?" He tried to look casual.

The waiter came back with a tray of coffee cups that were distributed and Henry asked to have one as well. The man moved quickly to fetch it recognizing the Mayor's aide.

"Remember the Saint Lorenzo celebration that was to happen last August on the saint's day?"

"I wasn't working in the North End then," Brendan said, taking a sip from his cup.

"First, there was a fire in the vestry, so they rescheduled. Then it got rained out. Hailed out. Instead of putting it together the following week—rain again—they decided to do it on the half-year anniversary." He looked at Amanda. "I'll bet you've never seen one of these events."

She shook her head.

"It's a religious parade through the neighborhood. They take the statue of the saint on a platform and selected men —it's a tremendous honor to be chosen—carry the saint through the streets."

"I'd like to see that," Amanda said.

"You just might if you're around on Thursday. That's when it will happen."

"So, is the Mayor going to join the walk?"

Henry looked around to see if anyone outside of his tablemates was listening. He stopped abruptly as the waiter reappeared with his cup and saucer, and Henry waited until he had walked away before resuming.

"The Mayor wants to, but then there is the matter of the Black Shirts."

Caroline asked, "Who are they?"

"The fascists. They call themselves the Fascist League of America. Big Mussolini supporters. Father Palladino and they are...." Here he crossed his fingers indicating they were very close.

"Not unusual," José said. "In my country the government and the Church are hand in glove. It's how everybody knows their place."

Henry took a swig out of his cup and smiled. "Good coffee here. I salute you."

José smiled. "That's one good thing my country is known for. Excellent coffee."

Henry's head swiveled to look back at the private room from which he had recently emerged. Out came the Police Chief, Morelli and several other men.

"They're trying to mitigate what could be a nasty situation. There is another faction that is adamantly opposed to Mussolini although they have been more underground. We don't even know who is involved."

"Are the Black Shirts that out in the open?" Amanda asked.

Henry waggled his hand from side to side. "Yes and no. We're getting whispers that Salvatore De Luca may be part of that group."

"But I thought he and the Mayor got along?" Amanda asked.

"In public, yes. But if he shows up at the next event with a cadre of thugs, the Mayor will kiss him goodbye as a Ward Heeler, no matter what his influence."

Brendan smiled. "De Luca has been working hard at cementing his position. Things could get interesting."

Rob shook his head and got up. "I don't care what anyone believes. I just don't want them getting in the way of commerce. Namely, mine."

"That's the American way," Brendan said with a smile.

Rob shrugged his shoulders and left to attend to some issue at the front entrance.

Henry gulped down the rest of his drink as he saw his boss approaching. "You'll find out. I'm sure you're going to be front and center along with a squad of plainclothes guys. Arrivederci," he said, getting up to meet his boss.

The Mayor and Morelli, both elegantly dressed, stopped by the table and Mr. Morelli nodded at Amanda.

"I don't believe we have been introduced," he said.

Amanda could feel the alert tension from Brendan as she smiled and said, "No."

"Antonio Morelli," he said with a slight bow and holding out his hand.

"Amanda Burnside," she replied, shaking his.

"And of course, I know the Honorable Brendan Halloran," he said, nodding at him. "You are in safe hands." He turned away, stopped and turned back. "And thank you for all that you do with the clinic. It makes a big difference to many people who can't afford going to the doctor for every ailment."

Amanda blushed. "You're welcome. My pleasure." She could feel Brendan's eyes drilling into her, warning her, but she didn't care. This elegantly dressed man with exquisite manners didn't seem to be a threat at all.

The lights at the raised stage dimmed and the first strains of a bluesy song began before the spotlight picked out Sofia in a long white dress and a flower in her hair. It was the typical man-who-done-me-wrong song, and she delivered it as if she really meant it.

"I think Rob is too involved with his business to notice what is going on sometimes," Brendan observed.

"That may be why he and Louisa get along so well. She is not at all interested in the business," Amanda said and stopped short when she recalled the shoebox with the pile of debts owed. She wondered if Louisa had even bothered to look inside the box.

They sat through Sofia's set and Amanda had a hard time concealing a yawn.

"Long day, eh?" Brendan asked.

"Yes, and long day tomorrow, too."

"Then let's go. I'm a working stiff, as you well know. If people see us leaving, they'll assume we are club hopping rather than almost dozing."

They said goodnight to Caroline and José, retrieved their coats and waited in the foyer while one of the turbaned men took off at a trot to fetch the car. Even wrapped in her warm coat with a pair of gloves, she felt the cold and shivered.

"I'll turn the heat up high," Brendan said and smiled at her.

They encountered more cars than anticipated on the way home, but the delay afforded the opportunity for the interior to warm up.

"That Henry is certainly something," Amanda said.

"What kind of something?"

"How can he possibly know all of things he suggests he has knowledge of?"

"He does get out and about. The former Mayor and staff tended to isolate themselves in the office and consequently didn't feel the winds shifting. He thought the criticism he read in the papers was just the journalists picking on him when, in reality, it was the murmurings of the people."

"You think that's why he was voted out?" Amanda asked.

"That and thinking that he was some kind of George Washington figurehead who looked like a Mayor and therefore should continue in office. He had the support of the Old Guard business community; they can supply campaign funds, but they have a limited number of votes. It didn't help that he put very little effort into reaching out to the newer voters in our fair city."

Amanda digested this information and realized that he was saying the old Yankee families were limited in number and the immigrants kept coming in and wanted to have their needs recognized. Like having a clinic in their neighborhood. This Mayor certainly knew how to get things done.

"Here we are," Brendan said, pulling up under a tree near the front of her house. He turned the ignition off and turned toward her. "I've had a lovely—if short—evening with you. And I hope we can do this or something else again."

"All right," she said.

"I do need to ask you something, however."

"Yes?"

"May I kiss you?"

She was trying to formulate an answer when he leaned over, put his hand behind her head gently and kissed her on the mouth. She tried not to gasp in surprise. He pulled back.

"That was nice," he said.

She didn't know how to respond and realized he wasn't expecting a response but was getting out of the car to open the passenger door. He put her arm through his and walked her to the front door.

"Thank you," he said, and she managed a smile while taking out her key and letting herself in. She stood for a moment in the foyer taking in what had just happened. That was no Fred-like kiss, for one thing. The other thing was that she felt as if she were floating on air.

## Chapter 18

Despite her whirling emotions and thoughts, she slept heavily that night and woke to the sounds of breakfast in the room one story beneath hers. Looking at the alarm clock, which she had forgotten to set, she gasped and hurriedly dressed and combed through what remained of the waves in her hair.

"How was your evening?" her mother asked.

"Very interesting. We went to the Oasis, Rob's club, and there was very stimulating conversation." She sat and poured herself some coffee.

"Really?" her father commented. "I didn't think the atmosphere in a nightclub was one of conversation."

"What did you imagine it would be? Wild dancing and singing?"

He chuckled. "I've never been, so it's all my imagination. Aside from what you see in movies."

"It's rather like that. People dressed up, acting sophisticated. A band, a singer."

"Alcohol?" her mother asked.

"I didn't ask for any," she said, cleverly disguising the fact that it had been set before her without her having to ask. "The interior is meant to look like some kind of Arabian scene with paintings of sand dunes on the walls and potted palms."

"What—no camels?" her father asked.

"No, and no pink elephants, either."

That got a laugh from him. "Maybe not while you were there but hours later."

"I can't believe I overslept. I must hurry over for the second day of the clinic."

"Do you think that's a good idea? Being around sick people? Especially children. I remember when you first started school and all the colds and childhood diseases you brought home," Mrs. Burnside said.

"I've been working in a hospital setting all along, Mother."

"But in an office, not on the wards."

"It's only temporary. Miss Bailey, who was meant to help register the people who came in, has been sick. Even if she's not better by next week, I'll get someone else to do that task. I'm better used elsewhere." She swallowed the last of her toast and got up. "Sorry to rush out like this," she said and went quickly upstairs to finish getting ready.

It was a sunny day at long last, although still cold. Her mind was half on the traffic and half on Brendan Halloran. Was he remembering last night in the same way she was? Or was that his usual goodnight to anyone he took out on a date? She shook her head to clear it and drove on.

Amanda arrived at the Sons of Italy Hall a mere ten minutes before the clinic was to open and was relieved there was no line outside the building. But walking down the stairs to the basement, she realized that about a dozen women were already seated, waiting for things to begin.

She took off her coat and gloves, leaving her hat on since it was still chilly in the building and went over to ask who had been first to come in, giving each a receipt and moving among them to complete the registration. She could hear more people coming in and thought that word must have circulated through the neighborhood after the previous day's clinic, a good sign. It didn't appear that anyone was afraid to come in or suspected that there was some nefarious government scheme at work. This group was noisier since there were two infants who were alternately whimpering or crying and some toddlers squirming in their mothers' laps.

Fred came out from behind one of the partitions and, seeing Amanda, tried a smile. "There you are."

"Yes, here I am. We've got a good turnout already. If you're ready, we can begin," she added.

"Good idea," he said, and she read out the name of a woman who took herself and the baby in behind the partition. Doctor Wilkinson came out from behind the other partition and got his patient. And so it went for several hours, a constant stream of mothers and children, most looking relieved when they left to at least have a diagnosis of what might be the matter.

Amanda looked at her watch and it was only eleven, but she was famished, having eaten a tiny breakfast, and not being scheduled to break for lunch until one o'clock. She caught the eye of one of the nurses and let her know that she was just popping up to the street and would return with cookies for them all. That promise bought her the license to trot up the stairs and head for the bakery that Henry had introduced her to.

She held the door open for a mother with a baguette in paper and a young child held by the hand and greeted the woman behind the counter. She decided to ask for an espresso and listened to the noisy ritual of its preparation while taking in all the varieties of cookies and baked goods. While she sipped the coffee, she pointed to what she wanted indicating with fingers how many of each—although the woman probably spoke English—and watched her put them in a pink box. Maybe Fred wouldn't be so grumpy after being fortified with some of these delicacies.

Amanda felt alert and energized and realized there was something to that drink that the weak coffee of home could not compare with. She went back to the hall with her haul of goodies that she put in the kitchen since there would not be enough for the women patiently waiting in the main room and discreetly told the nurses of the bounty.

The ebb and flow of women and children—and there was not a single man to be seen—continued until almost noon and then died down as people were at home having their lunch. She wondered if she should go to Catalano's again or perhaps try another place and whom she could ask for a recommendation. There was a crash of doors and a woman's shouting and wailing coming down the stairs. Amanda went to the stairwell to see what was going on, hoping that it wasn't some medical emergency that they couldn't handle. But it was Mrs. Rinaldi with just a sweater over her dress calling for help.

"What is it?" Amanda asked as the women present surrounded her.

She spoke rapidly in Italian, and the women asked her questions to which she responded with great vigor and anger.

"What is it?" Amanda repeated.

"She says her daughter has eloped with Santoro," one of them said.

"How does she know?"

"She said she didn't show up for her job this morning."

"Is she of age to get married without her parents' consent?"

Mrs. Rinaldi glared at Amanda and spit out the word, "Si!"

The group became silent.

"I don't know if anything can be done if she is old enough to get married on her own," Amanda said.

"She's been kidnapped!" Mrs. Rinaldi said. "Call the police!"

Amanda thought the mother made this up on the spot to get someone in authority involved to resolve what was essentially a family problem. Still, she had Mrs. Rinaldi sit down and she went upstairs to a telephone and called the police, explaining the situation and got the response that someone would be there right away. That turned out to be more like twenty minutes, in which time Mrs. Rinaldi had poured out her story to the women, alternately weeping and railing, while they tried to soothe her. Fred and Wilkinson came out from behind the partitions to see what the matter was, and Amanda explained it as best she could.

Minutes later, Halloran and Dominic came crashing down the stairs and the fierce look in their eyes pierced her heart. Dominic quizzed the mother in Italian, translating to Halloran in bits and pieces.

"Does she know for sure that a kidnapping has occurred?"

"She's adamant that's what happened." Dominic turned away from the women and looked at Halloran with an expression that indicated that he doubted it and shrugged his shoulders. "We can always check in on Marco and then his apartment in the event she's holed up there. Maybe Angela is just trying to get away from the drama at home."

"Good call," Halloran said. "Let's go." They went back upstairs and out to their car parked half on the sidewalk outside. "Stupid fools," he muttered.

They got to the dockside in a matter of minutes and left the car blocking any other vehicular traffic while they went in search of Marco.

"Where's Santoro?" Dominic asked the boss. He jutted his thumb over his shoulder.

They went in that direction and saw that he was loading crates and writing on them with chalk.

"What do you want now?" he snarled at them.

"Where's Angela?"

"I don't know. Probably at work." His animosity turned to concern when he realized that something might be amiss. "What's wrong?"

"Is she at your place? Maybe with your mother?"

"No. Not that I know of. I can't get off work to look. You know where my mother lives."

"Yes," Dominic said, and they quickly left, with Marco looking worried, before his boss walked over and told him to get back to work.

Halloran and Dominic sped to the Santoro apartment, remembering that the mother worked the night shift and would be home. They pounded on her door, but it was a few minutes before the groggy woman wrapped in a robe came to the door.

"What do you want now?" she said as she opened it and looked at the two men.

"Have you seen Angela Rinaldi?"

"What? No. I've been sleeping."

"Do you mind if we search the apartment?"

"For what?'

"For the girl," Dominic said.

She plopped herself on the sofa in the front room with her head in her hands while they searched the few rooms including the closets and found nobody there.

"Was she here?" they asked when they came back into the front room.

"Of course not. What do you think, we have tea parties together or something? Her family can't stand my son and so I don't think much of them. I don't know where they meet or when they meet or nothing. Marco tells me nothing, and I don't ask."

"Okay," Halloran said, and they made for the door. As he closed it, she yelled out behind them.

"You're welcome."

They clattered down the stairs.

"Now what?" Dominic asked.

"Let's go talk to Rinaldi. Maybe he can shed some light on this. Just because she missed work doesn't mean something terrible has happened."

"Maybe she and Marco are going to elope, and she's at a girlfriend's place until he gets off work."

"Could be. That's in a few hours. Let's talk to Rinaldi and then circle back for when Marco gets off work and see where he goes.

When they got to the religious shop, Mr. Rinaldi was assisting a customer, but his eyes were wide with fear when he saw the two detectives come in.

"I'll be with you gentlemen in a moment," he said, pretending they were customers waiting their turn. The woman he was assisting was making up her mind on which missal she should buy for an upcoming communion, and the detectives and Rinaldi were getting impatient with her indecision.

"All right. I think this one. It's more expensive, but she's my goddaughter after all. Her parents will recognize the quality."

"Yes, indeed," Rinaldi said, moving quickly to the counter and wrapping it in brown paper while she fished in her handbag for a coin purse.

"Can't you gift wrap it?"

If she heard the frustrated sigh of the detectives, she didn't acknowledge it in any way and patiently waited while Rinaldi searched under the counter for gift wrapping. Dominic went to the workshop, found nobody there, then wandered around the store picking up items and looking at the prices. Finally, the missal was paid for, and the woman left the shop.

"Your wife has reported your daughter missing. Is she here?" Halloran asked.

"No. She is missing?"

"Didn't you wife tell you?"

He stammered. "She said Angela didn't get to work this morning."

"Why does she think she is missing? What was going on in your house that your wife thinks that?"

Mr. Rinaldi had drops of sweat on his forehead. "Nothing. Everything was as it should be." He glanced at the Madonna behind the counter.

Halloran walked around the shop and picked up a few items, pretending to look at the prices but remembering Amanda's comment, he was scanning the wall toward the back where it didn't meet the adjacent one at exactly the right angle. Old buildings had their quirks, but something about that intrigued him and he put down the scapular he had been holding and walked back to the workshop, noting the closed off space between the two areas. He came back into the shop itself and saw Rinaldi's large eyes following him.

"What's that space between the shop and the back?"

Rinaldi shrugged his shoulders. I don't know. Maybe pipes go through it. Or what they call a bearing wall."

Halloran began to knock on the wall which sounded hollow.

"It's been like that since I moved in," Rinaldi said quickly.

Halloran continued tapping as he moved along. "You don't know what's behind here?"

Rinaldi was moving toward the detective, intent on stopping him. Viewing it as a potential attack, Dominic thrust himself over the counter, knocking Rinaldi down against the wall behind the counter, and the Madonna overhead crashed to the ground, the plaster shattering in pieces.

"What are you doing? What have you done?" Rinaldi cried out, snatching at the pieces.

Halloran had moved quickly to catch up with the activity behind the counter and scowled at Dominic, thinking his tackle had been excessive. After all, Rinaldi, being older, pudgy and out of shape, was hardly a physical threat to either of the detectives. Halloran winced as he crushed a piece of plaster under his feet in his haste, then realized the statue was beyond repair. He bent to pick up a small cloth bag with a red star on it just as Rinaldi scrabbled for it.

"What's this?" He undid the drawstring and unfurled a paper.

"That must have dropped from the counter," Rinaldi said. "Don't read it!"

"I can't read it. It's in Italian," Halloran said, giving it to Dominic.

"Yes, but it doesn't make any sense. Just a bunch of sentences."

"What does it say?"

"'Flowers arrive.' Or come soon. Um, 'boats are blue.' What does that mean? And 'love to Mama.'"

"Code of some kind? Intended for whom?" Halloran asked.

Rinaldi snatched it from Dominic's hand and was about to stuff it in his mouth, but the detective stopped him. Halloran stepped back and slipped on a piece of plaster which sent him careening into the wall he had recently been tapping on and felt it give way. He got his balance and asked Rinaldi again, "What's behind that wall?" Getting no answer, he kicked at the wall with his foot, and it swung inward on hinges revealing a long space that was a few feet wide. He squeezed himself into it and pulled some papers from a shelf and emerged.

"What's this?"

Dominic answered for him. "Anti-fascist leaflets."

Rinaldi began to cry.

"Hey, we've got First Amendment protections in this country. As long as you don't intend to overthrow it, you're okay." Then he added, "For the most part."

"They have my daughter," Rinaldi said. "They called me."

"What? Who?"

"The fascists have my daughter. They know something in this shop contained a message and they must have thought Giovanni knew where it was. They were looking in the plaster statues in the workroom when he interrupted them."

"Why didn't they look in the Madonna behind the counter?" Dominic asked.

"She wasn't here. Someone from our side is supposed to come, give me the sign of the red star and take her. But nobody has come." He sniffed and wiped his nose with a handkerchief. "I can't leave her here overnight, so I take her home every day and hide her in a closet. My wife doesn't know about any of this. She thinks I do this because it is a valuable piece—and it is. But not in the way she thinks. I didn't feel well the morning Giovanni was assassinated and that's why I hadn't come into the shop yet. If only I had!" He began crying again.

"If you had been here, both of you would have been killed." Halloran helped the man to his feet. "When did these people call? And what did they say?"

"They said they wanted the message, or they would kill her."

"Are they going to contact you again?"

"Yes, this evening. At six o'clock."

"Did they speak in English or Italian?"

"Italian, of course."

"Dominic, why don't you go to their place about five in case they call early. And listen in on the conversation. Do you know what the message means?" he asked Rinaldi.

"No."

"Good. Then in the meantime, we'll need to concoct a different message."

Rinaldi stared at him.

"When you talk to them tonight, agree to meet them some-where—not at your apartment. In fact, let them set the meeting place so we'll be able to see them or follow them."

"I'm scared," Rinaldi said.

"We'll be with you," Halloran said, patting him on the back. "I guess you'd better close for the day. Take the message home with you. Don't tell your wife what's going on, okay?"

Rinaldi nodded and went to lock the door and pull down the shade.

"Who in your group is supposed to pick up the message?"

Rinaldi turned and stared. "I don't know. Someone will come to get it and leave me a sign."

"Oh, okay. I get it. Is that Marco involved with the fascists? Is that why you don't like him?"

"No. I just don't like him. His family is from Palermo."

# Chapter 19

The last person had been seen at the clinic and the janitor was already beginning to put the chairs away. One of the nurses came out to the table where Amanda sat and said, "Whew! What a day. What happened to the mother? Did she find her daughter?"

"I don't know," Amanda said. "She might have been exaggerating about the kidnapping part because the families don't get along."

"Romeo and Juliet," the nurse said.

"Something like that. If they're resolving it with an elopement, let's hope it's a better outcome that the original story."

"These people are so emotional," the nurse whispered and went back to the kitchen to pack up their equipment.

Fred had just washed his hands and taken off his white coat as he approached Amanda's chair. "I guess you've proved your point about there being a need for children's services here. I'd be interested to know if the attendance at the main clinic was less during this time."

"Meaning some who would have gone there came here? It's still cold and flu season, so perhaps not. Where do you think our next outpost should be?" she asked.

He held out both hands. "Stop! Not so soon. We haven't even got into a rhythm yet. It's our first week."

"I was just pulling your leg. We still have to get someone to do the intake. I thought about getting a volunteer from the neighborhood and then considered that there might be a problem with privacy or gossip. But if one of the hospital volunteers does it, that won't be an issue."

"I'm glad I was in on the pilot program to assess what kind of space, equipment and staff we need," Fred said. "But I can't continue in this role. There's too much waiting back at Mercy for me."

"I understand. But you're not going to recommend scuttling it entirely, are you?"

"I'll have to give it some thought," Fred said, turning to get his belongings.

Amanda was astonished. Was he going to sabotage what she had worked so hard to get going? Was that his rational mind at work or was he just exhausted? Or was he trying to sink her efforts?

She made a lot of noise packing up her things and left without saying goodbye. All the way home she turned over in her mind what motivations might be at work for Fred Browne. Was he jealous of her achievements? Or just plain jealous?

She stepped outside to the bustle of activity getting ready for the next day's celebration. Merchants along Hanover Street had hung small Italian flags and pennants and there was more pedestrian traffic than usual as residents wanted to see what might be in store the next day.

Amanda got home well before four o'clock and took herself into the kitchen to make a cup of tea. Cook was busy basting a roast and Simona had just walked in.

"Hello, Miss," she said brightly.

Cook turned around. "Good afternoon, Miss."

"I just wanted some tea. And sympathy."

"What ails you?" Cook asked.

"Bruised ego, I think. I thought the clinic in the North End was a success, but the doctors and nurses might not feel the same. There were quite a lot of people, more than they are used to seeing in a day. That just means there is a need for that kind of service in the neighborhoods."

"That's all people were talking about last night," Simona said.

"Really? In a good way, I hope."

"Of course."

"Then you should be proud of your work," Cook said.

"I am. I think someone was just grumpy."

"A name?" Cook asked.

Amanda made a motion of twisting a key in a lock of her lips and tossing away he invisible key. Cook and Simona both laughed.

"But the real excitement was Mrs. Rinaldi coming in claiming her daughter had eloped with the boyfriend the family doesn't like."

"The future mother-in-law always objects. It's a tradition. It sets up high expectations that the man can never meet," Simona said.

"That sounds awful," Cook said.

Simona shrugged. "Old Country customs. Because the man takes the daughter away to his house. It's a loss for the family."

"Oh, you've made madeleines," Amanda said, seeing them cooling on a rack.

"Sit down, here's your tea, and you are welcome to them."

Amanda obeyed, accepted the cup and saucer, took a cookie and savored the still warm delicacy. "The other excitement was anticipating the Saint Lorenzo celebration."

Simona rolled her eyes.

"What?" Amanda asked.

"It's going to be an opportunity for all kinds of political nonsense. I heard some men are going to march with black shirts on," Simona said.

Cook looked puzzled. "Some costume—but what's wrong with that?"

"Fascists, that's what."

"I thought Italians favored anarchists, like that Sacco and his partner who robbed the company a few years ago."

"That was a complicated case," Simona said. "Anyway, people in Italy might like Il Duce, but that's for them to decide. I don't think Americans should get involved in their politics. Didn't people have enough of that during the Great War?"

Cook raised her eyebrows. "You seem to know a lot about history. But then, you got to graduate from high school. Some of us weren't so lucky. I had to go to work to support the family." She sniffed and tended to something on the stove.

"I worked at my family's restaurant while I was going to school," Simona responded in a quiet voice.

Sensing the tension building, Amanda complimented Cook on the madeleines and took her cup and saucer with her into her father's study to make a telephone call.

"Detective Halloran, please," she said to the operator, and she was connected immediately.

He sounded brusque as he answered, "Halloran."

"Brendan, I saw you today and know that you were in quite a rush, but was the Rinaldis' daughter found?" He didn't respond immediately, and she followed up with, "It caused quite a stir with the patients at the clinic."

"I imagine it did," he answered.

There was another awkward pause where she expected him to say something, but he was silent.

"Have you got any closer to solving who killed that poor Giovanni?" she asked.

"No, and you know I can't possibly discuss that with a civilian. You ought to stick to the clinic side of things."

She hung up without saying more. "Of all the nerve!" she said out loud. "I was there shortly after it happened!"

"After what happened?" her mother said, putting her head into the room. "And what are you doing in here? This stuffy, pipe smoke-filled den that your father inhabits to get away from the womenfolk." She went to a window and struggled to open it. "I'll bet this hasn't been opened in years."

"Let me," Amanda said. With a tremendous yank, she was able to open the lower sash and the cold air rushed in. "It may be freezing, but at least it's fresh."

"Who were you talking to?"

"Myself, actually. I may have overestimated somebody." She gave her mother a tight smile and left to stew in her bedroom.

HALLORAN REGRETTED his sharp comment to Amanda and was about to call her back with a lame apology when the Chief appeared in the doorway, so he put the receiver back.

"Sir?" he asked, standing up.

The Chief waved his hand to indicate the detective should not stand on ceremony. "What the devil is going on in that neighborhood?" he asked.

"That's just how it is there. People get all het up about any little thing."

"First, there's the smoke bomb thing that got the Mayor all a-twitter, now someone is yowling about a kidnapping. Is the whole neighborhood going to hell in a handbasket?"

"We're working on the kidnapping or elopement, depending upon how you look at it. There may be some political issues behind the recent events."

The Chief looked down his long nose at Halloran. "Maybe you should step back and let Dominic take the reins on this."

"He and I have been working together. I'm sure we'll come to some conclusion soon."

The Chief took his index finger and ran it along the edge of Halloran's desk. "One more week and then we'll see if you aren't better used somewhere else in the city." He could see Halloran's intense look.

"Take it easy, boyo. It just means that we value your talent. And what's this nonsense of them having some kind of religious parade?"

"Saint Lorenzo. They couldn't do it on the usual saint's day due to weather and something else. So, De Luca and Palladino have re-scheduled for the half-year anniversary."

The Chief rolled his eyes. "I wish they'd keep those primitive customs out of our city. Jesus, Mary and Joseph, we're Catholics, too, but we don't need to parade a statue in the streets to prove it. They've asked me to attend. I'll be at home, thank you, although I told them I had an important meeting. You and Dominic should both be there, in addition to the uniforms, in case there is any trouble." He knocked twice on the desk and winked before he left.

"Gee, thanks," Halloran muttered when he was out of earshot.

## Chapter 20

Dominic got to the Rinaldis' apartment, not looking forward to sitting with the nervous father waiting for a telephone call, so he was surprised that it was his wife who opened the door.

"Have you found them yet?" she asked.

Dominic was puzzled and looked over her shoulder to see her husband shaking his head warning him not to say more.

"Not quite, but we've got a good lead." She didn't understand what the last word meant so he translated it for her, and the rest of their conversation was in Italian.

She smiled. "Come in, you must be hungry," and she propelled him to the small table in the kitchen where she had been rolling out gnocchi. His eyes widened.

"Doesn't your mama make these?" she asked.

"Not enough."

She laughed and continued the deft rolling of the pieces of dough on a small, ridged board. "You'll stay for supper, yes?"

"Yes, indeed."

"Take off your coat," she urged him, and he went back to the living room where he had left his hat. Rinaldi was sitting on the sofa reading a newspaper.

"I haven't told her anything except that we are working on a deal and will have a private conversation with someone on the telephone at six o'clock. I told her she had to go in the bedroom while we talk on the phone," Rinaldi said.

That sounded awkward to Dominic, but it would have to work. He went back to the kitchen and found that Mrs. Rinaldi had poured him a small glass of red wine. She smiled sheepishly at him.

"Do policemen make good money?" she asked him in Italian.

"Good enough," he answered.

"And you live with your parents?"

"Yes."

"My Angela is a good girl," she continued.

"I'm sure she is," Dominic said noncommittally since the conversation was starting to sound like she was veering into matchmaking territory. Sure, he could be the knight in shining armor who brought the purloined princess back to the family. And as his reward? An engagement! He tried to think of something to say to change the topic that wouldn't remind her of her son's death. "Are you going to the festival tomorrow?"

"Sure. Funny you should ask. Saint Lorenzo is the patron saint of chefs. So here we are," she said, motioning at the last of the gnocchi she had made. She stepped over to the stove and removed the lid from a pot and he smelled the garlic in the red sauce as she stirred it. "I've made stuffed artichokes, too," she said over her shoulder.

Dominic sighed. One of his favorites and very labor-intensive.

"They'll be ready soon."

"Are you tiring him out?" Rinaldi asked from the living room.

"I'm just keeping her company," he responded.

"Well, come in here."

Dominic took his wine into the living room, sat down in a chair, picked up a section of the newspaper and tried to read it. Although he was fluent, his reading skills in the foreign language weren't very good and the article he was trying to read had to do with agrarian reforms in Italy.

The telephone rang and Rinaldi shot out of his chair. "Mama, into the bedroom. Now!"

She turned the gas burners on the stove off and scurried down the hall as the phone rang again. He waited until the door was closed before he picked up the phone with Dominic's ear on the other side of the receiver.

"Hello!" he shouted.

"Tomorrow. At the festival. Bring it."

"Where? To where?"

"You'll find out then."

They hung up.

"Where is she?" Rinaldi said to the dial tone, hung up the phone and slumped onto the sofa. He put his head in his hands. "What do we do now?"

"What he said. I've already written another message to put in the bag."

Rinaldi held out his hand.

"I'll give it to you tomorrow. We must be very careful. These folks could be dangerous. Detective Halloran will be there, and we'll have two more guys with us."

"Antonio!" Mrs. Rinaldi shouted from the bedroom. "Antonio!"

"Yes, yes, you can come out," he shouted back to her.

She moved quickly to the kitchen and relit the burners. "The dinner will be ruined with your nonsense of secret calls," she said. "Now I have to start the water boiling all over again."

Dominic was glad that she was preoccupied with the meal and couldn't see her husband's face, grey with worry.

## Chapter 21

Amanda saw a police wagon parked at the end of Hanover Street and wondered if there had been some kind of disturbance before she realized that was how they had transported eight policemen to assist with the procession. It wasn't due to start for another hour, but sawhorses were in place preventing vehicular traffic, which meant that she had to park her car far from the Sons of Italy Hall, where musicians were assembling. The men who would be transporting the statue of the saint would start off from the church.

People were already lining the streets and vendors had set up pushcarts to sell lemonade, cookies and ices even though it was another cold day. She had the foresight to wear wool trousers and a warm sweater under her coat, anticipating a long time standing. Across the street she saw Halloran and Dominic, waved to them and trotted across the road.

"Gosh, what are you doing here?" she asked. "And I saw so many policemen already."

"The Mayor insisted on having our crack team here." He pointed to himself and Halloran not looing pleased to have got the assignment. "After all the disturbances at last year's Saint Paddy's Day parade, you never know."

"I didn't hear about that," Amanda said.

"No, you wouldn't have. The powers that be wanted to keep it quiet so folks wouldn't think there were mobs in the streets. It would have only been a few drunks, but then the Orangemen showed up," Halloran explained.

"Who are they?"

The two detectives looked at each other.

"I think you need to get out more," Halloran said with a smirk.

Amanda turned away, feeling foolish at her lack of knowledge.

"We're not here to watch the procession, we're here to work. Maybe we'll see you later," he said to her back.

Not wanting to stand outside in the cold, Amanda retreated to the bakery, which was open and warm as usual. She ordered an espresso and chatted with the woman behind the counter who pointed out some freshly baked cookies covered in powdered sugar that she bought and stashed in her handbag. As she sat sipping her drink, the number of people outside increased, and the police stood in the street restricting the crowds to the sidewalk.

"You've come for the procession?" the woman asked her.

"Yes, I've never seen it before."

"It's very special to us. I'll be closing in a while to watch." She waved Amanda down with her hand. "Stay, stay, I'll let you know when. It's too cold to be outside for long. My poor husband is out there with his cart and that's why things here look bare. He'll sell them all, I'm sure. And then go to bed with a hot water bottle for the evening." She laughed.

The minutes went by and, despite the woman's statement, she felt she had overstayed her welcome and got up to go.

"Listen! You can hear the musicians!" the woman said, disappearing into the back. A few moments later, she came out, wrapping a woolen scarf around her head and putting on a thick coat.

It wasn't as cold as earlier, perhaps because there were so many people blocking the wind. Amanda, taller than most women and some men, could easily see over the heads of the people standing in front of her. In the distance she could hear the rat-a-tat of drums and horns being played. The people were craning their necks to look and an errant child who stepped into the street was told to return to the sidewalk by a stern policeman. He didn't see the child stick out his tongue, but Amanda heard the smack the boy received from his mother and the subsequent yelp.

The musicians were moving slowly, not really walking, but processing, taking one step forward and then bringing the other foot in alignment for a beat. The music was loud, percussive and at the same time sad, almost like a dirge. As they moved closer to where Amanda stood, she could see that it was a small group and that they were followed by De Luca and several other men dressed in suits with tricolor sashes stretching diagonally from shoulder to waist. They were solemn and walked in that same halting manner.

Next came a cluster of adult women dressed formally, and Amanda wondered if these were the wives of the men who came walked ahead or if there was some female honorary group associated with the church, perhaps an altar society. Following them was another band of musicians, dressed in white shirts with decorated vests and embroidered caps that she assumed were a regional costume. Then came a school group carrying a banner with Saint Lorenzo's School emblazoned on it. Another group of musicians followed them at a distance, then a troupe of dancers—the same that performed for the previous celebration; however, this time they walked rather than danced swishing their skirts.

It seemed every possible group, school, club and association had taken part in the procession, and she wondered how there could still be so many people on the sidewalk, now pushing and shoving a bit to get a better look. Amanda felt a tug and then realized a figure that darted past her had grabbed the handbag out of her hands.

"Stop! Thief! He stole my handbag!" she yelled and tried to make her way through the mass of people. "Stop him!" But everyone was looking in the other direction and nobody paid attention to her cries.

She tapped a policeman on the shoulder and shouted, "That boy stole my handbag."

"Sorry lady, I can't help. Got to do crowd control."

She stamped her foot in annoyance and saw that the young man who had taken her purse had darted across the street and into an alley. There wasn't much money in it, but it contained her car keys and her driver's license, so she pushed through the people in front and ran across the street, too, while the policeman whom she had asked for assistance shouted for her to get out of the street.

The young man might have been younger than she, but her legs were longer and once he had disappeared into the alley, he slowed down and opened the purse to inspect the contents. The last thing he expected was this tall woman barreling down the alley with a ferocious look on her face. He dropped the handbag and ran down the alley and jumped over the low wall at the end.

He had spilled some of the contents onto the ground but hadn't taken her money and luckily not her car keys, but there was a mess of broken cookies and powdered sugar, so she shook the crumbs out and she shoveled everything else back in to walk back toward Hanover Street.

There was a thumping noise and a muffled woman's voice cried out.

Amanda looked up and around and saw nobody at first, then a face at a basement window that jerked in the direction of a grimy door at the top of a few steps. She hesitated but could see that the woman was distressed, and her cries were urgent so she went over and yanked on the doorknob and found herself in a dark hallway that smelled of boiled cabbage or something worse. She looked to her right and found another door, opened it and went down the cement steps to another door that was surprisingly unlocked. It led to a dingy basement room. It took a moment to adjust her eyes to the gloom, but then she was startled to see a young woman who was standing on a chair, her hands bound in front of her, a gag around her face waiting by the window.

"What's going on?" Amanda said rushing over to remove the gag.

"Please hurry, they'll be back soon."

"Who? What?"

There were noises coming from above and the woman, who was no more than a teenage girl, opened her eyes wide and said, "They're coming back. Quick, hide."

Amanda's eyes scanned the room. "Hide where?" There was a bed in the corner with a jumble of blankets and she thought she might be able to make herself invisible in the blankets. Stupid idea—instead she pulled the blankets that hung over the side away and shimmied herself under the bed. No sooner was she there, than she regretted her choice as the floor was filthy and smelled terrible. But for the moment she was safe.

"Hey, what are you doing!" a man's voice shouted to the girl. "Get back on the bed or we'll have to tie you up." She protested but they threw her on the bed and her weight smashed into Amanda underneath who let out an involuntary grunt.

"What's that?"

A short man with a menacing face pulled back the blankets and looked under the bed. "Get out of there!"

Amanda obeyed and in one sense was happy to be out of the dust and dirt as she brushed down her clothes.

"Who the hell are you?" he sneered.

"I may ask the same of you," she said loftily.

He grabbed her arm.

"Let go of me," she said and initially he did, then realized he had the upper hand and grabbed her again.

"Sit down!"

"Why is this girl tied up? What is she doing down here? Who is she?"

"None of your business. You're staying down here, too. I gotta figure this out." He got up and closed and locked the door, leaving the two women alone.

"What's your name?"

"Angela Rinaldi."

"Why have they taken you? And who has taken you?" Amanda tried to undo the rope tied around the girl's wrists but failed. "Wait a minute," she said, digging into her purse and pulling out a nail file. She got better purchase with the sharp metal than she could with her fingernails and the rope was quickly undone.

"Thank you."

"Who was that man?"

"I have no idea. But there were at least two of them and they grabbed me on my way into work while it was still dark out."

"But, why? Has this got anything to do with your brother's death?"

"I don't know. Maybe it's a vendetta against my family."

"Whatever it is, we've got to figure a way out of here. Have you ever picked a lock before?" Amanda asked.

"No," Angela answered forcefully.

"Well, now it as good a time as any to give it a try," and she took her nail file to the door and began jiggling around inside the lock.

# Chapter 22

The procession moved slowly down Hanover with Halloran on one side of the street and Dominic on the other about twenty feet away from Rinaldi, looking for any persons who might approach him. To their eyes, it seemed everyone was intent on the event, waiting for the statue of the saint to come into view. They could also see Rinaldi, standing prominently at the edge of the sidewalk, waiting for someone to contact him or search his pockets for the message. It was a cold day, but he was sweating profusely and his eyes were darting all around, searching.

Father Palladino came into view with a beatific smile on his face. He was followed by four altar boys, one swinging a censer and receiving a catcall from a boy from a second-story window. After them came a dozen boys and girls dressed in their white communion outfits, perhaps the star pupils of the parochial school. Then, several yards behind, was the statue of Saint Lorenzo, wobbling a bit on the plat-form as the eight men who had it hoisted on their padded shoulders walked in the same slow manner as those before them.

Dominic looked across at Halloran and they both shrugged their shoulders. Where was their guy? As the saint came forward, people fell to their knees and crossed themselves, both Dominic and Halloran reflexively doing the same. They looked back up quickly but the men carting the platform blocked their view. As soon as the saint had passed, the two detectives scanned the crowd on either side of the street and saw that Rinaldi was gone.

Halloran glared at Dominic, who shrugged his shoulders and then pointed down the street where two men, one on either side, were hustling Rinaldi through the crowd toward an alley. Halloran ran across the street, skirting the next musical group and, by staying in the street, made faster time gaining on Rinaldi and his abductors than Dominic, who was hampered by the throng. Halloran stopped when he reached the entrance to the alley and hesitated, not wanting to be seen by them, then quickly poked his head around to see where they were taking their victim. He saw a door open and retracted his head as one of the men looked back to see if anyone was following. They manhandled Rinaldi through the door, and it slammed shut.

Halloran looked back to see if Dominic was close, caught his eye and motioned into the alley before running toward the door, which was unlocked. He opened it slowly and could hear the noise of three large men trying to descend a staircase abreast behind a door to the right, stumbling as they got to the bottom. He heard keys jangling and scuffling and someone trying to get up the stairs amid shouts and women's screams before there was a thump. Then all was quiet.

He put his ear to the door and could hear another door being opened and a young woman cry out, "Papa!" The door was closed. Halloran turned around to see Dominic coming through the door to the alley panting.

"Shh! There are two of them. A short fat guy and a taller big guy. Which one do you want?"

"Give me the big guy. I've got a sap in my pocket," Dominic said.

They crept down the stairs, hearing an argument in progress with two women's voices berating the abductors.

"Animal!" one cried out.

"You touch me and I'll have the law on you in an instant," a more familiar voice said.

When they got to the bottom of the stairs, Halloran nodded to Dominic and gingerly tried the door to see if it was unlocked. He didn't want to break it down with his shoulder unless it was necessary. It was unlocked; these guys were very sloppy, and he hoped they were just as stupid. He nodded to Dominic, turned the knob and broke into the room.

The two men were standing over Rinaldi, who was sprawled out on the bed, moaning and holding his head. At the sound of someone breaking into the room, the other men turned, utterly surprised. Halloran was just as shocked to see Angela and Amanda standing nearby, but he only hesitated a moment before hurling himself at the short guy, who was very slow at reacting to the attack. Dominic had the sap in his hand and whacked the tall man on the side of the head. He crashed to the ground, the sound distracting the smaller man. Halloran twisted his arm behind his back and had a pair of handcuffs at the ready, clicking them in place. It was all over in a matter of minutes.

"What are you doing here?" he asked Amanda.

"I heard Angela calling for help." She pointed to the basement window that let dim light into the room.

"Why did they take me? What is this all about?"

"I think they're the ones who killed your brother," Halloran said.

Angela looked wildly around, took a big step back and kicked at the man on the floor with all her might. "Animal!" She let out a stream of Italian that had Dominic's eyebrows up before going to her father and pulling him upright.

"Let's get them out of here, the little guy as well. We can lock the big guy in the room since he's unconscious now. Give me the keys," Halloran said, then realizing his prisoner was handcuffed, reached into the man's pockets and pulled out a large ring. "Go up and get one of the uniformed men to call the station? The procession must be almost past by now."

Dominic raced up the stairs while Halloran escorted the prisoner as Angela hurled epithets at him the entire time as she assisted her father. They came out of the alley and could see the tail end of the procession going by with a phalanx of men in black shirts, marching with their chests out greeted by a combination of applause and derision. Someone hurled an object in their direction, and one of the marchers broke ranks and jumped into the crowd, followed by some of his brethren, and the solemn religious event broke into chaos.

"There'll be a full house at the station tonight, if I can get through this crowd to my car," Halloran said, leading Rinaldi, the prisoner and the two women away from the fray.

"I've got my car parked a few blocks away if yours is on the other end of the street."

"It's highly irregular. But it's been that sort of a day."

They made their way through crowds amassing to see who was fighting with whom to Amanda's car. Halloran, Rinaldi and the prisoner piled into the back, Angela in the front, looking back at her father who had banged his head in the earlier altercation.

"I'm all right," he said. "I think everything will be okay."

They drove to the station without further conversation, and Amanda had the idea that she would just drop everyone off and return home.

"No, you are a victim here, too. I intend to hit them with everything we've got."

Her shoulders slumped, envisioning hours of interviews, sitting on the uncomfortable wooden benches in the waiting room, sipping the awful coffee that was proffered and wondering if she could call her parents to let them know that she was all right, although they had no reason to suspect anything was wrong. She looked at her watch and realized it wasn't yet lunchtime and she had nothing else planned for the day. Selfishly, she hoped they would interview her first as she had the least to do with whatever had gone on, but Halloran and Dominic wanted to talk to Rinaldi.

"Did these guys even ask for the bag with the message?"

"No. They just grabbed me and dragged me to the basement."

The detectives looked at each other. "I'm thinking these thugs weren't fully informed as to what was going on. Just doing a job," Dominic said.

"Where is the real message?" Halloran asked.

"It's safe. In the cash register at the store. Locked up."

Halloran screwed up his face. "Anyone could have broken into the store during the procession. Give Dominic the keys and he can check that it's still there."

Rinaldi, whose head already ached, put it between his hands. "Stupido!"

Dominic left quickly.

"Did these men ask you any questions?"

"No, they hardly spoke. They grabbed me off the street and took me down the stairs. Are they the ones who killed my Giovanni?"

"It's likely, but we're not sure yet. Why don't you sit with your daughter while we start with those clowns."

Amanda was interviewed by a young officer who evidently didn't have much background in the case because he asked generic questions. She decided to interrupt him and tell her connection with the entire thing. It took time, and he was scribbling like mad but she finally got to the day's events.

"I was standing watching the procession and somebody grabbed my handbag. I gave pursuit and he dropped it and ran away. It was then that I heard Angela call for help from a basement window and I found my way inside and downstairs. The idiots who took her forgot to lock the door. I intended to untie her and get her out, but the chubby man came in and locked us both in. At least she got untied and she was able to tell me something of what had happened while I was trying to pick the lock with my nail file. It is not an efficient way of doing so, by the way. Then we heard commotion on the stairs and the two men brought her father crashing down the stairs before Brendan and Dominic arrived.

He looked up at her use of their first names.

"I know the two detectives," she said. She waited until he finished writing and said, "Can I go now?"

"I'll ask Detective Halloran," he said, and she sighed in exasperation.

A few minutes later, Halloran came into the interview room. "How are they treating you?"

Dominic burst into the room and stopped, seeing that Amanda was there.

"Did you find the message?" Halloran asked.

Amanda was puzzled, not knowing what they were talking about.

"This is strange. Someone got into the cash register. They didn't take any money, no damage was done to the store or workshop. They took the message and a star outlined in red was drawn on the counter."

Halloran thought for a moment. "It seems that the real message was retrieved by the person it was intended for. Whomever that was."

"What's this all about?" Amanda asked.

"Tell Rinaldi what you found," he said to Dominic, who left to do so.

"I hope you're not here to interview me. I just spent an inordinate amount of time reciting my involvement with this case to a young officer who scribbled as fast as he could," Amanda said.

"That's because you speak so fast," he said with a smile.

"Well, life is short."

He looked at her for a long moment and she became uncomfortable.

"What is it?" she asked.

"You saved my life before and today I saved yours. I've met your family. I think it's time that you met mine."

"Oh," was all she could manage. "I think we are about to enter on an entirely new sort of adventure."

"Yes, indeed," he said with a smile.

What's next for Amanda and Brendan? Obviously, she can't seem to stop stumbling into a murder investigation and a **MURDER AT CITY HALL** is no exception. Get it here on pre-order, due for release August 2023.

Help other readers find these books and leave a short review. Thank you.
SEE MORE AT MY WEBSITE

DON'T FORGET, **MURDER AT CITY HALL** is next in the Massachusetts Cozy Mystery Series.

HAPPY READING!

Made in United States
Troutdale, OR
09/06/2024

22627793R00126